ULYSSES' CAT

ULYSSES' CAT

New Writing from South-East
Europe and Wales

PARTHIAN

Parthian, Cardigan SA43 1ED
www.parthianbooks.com
© authors and translators
Print ISBN: 978-1-914595-59-2
Edited by Alexandra Büchler
Cover Design by Lyn Davies Design
Typeset by Elaine Sharples
Printed by 4Edge
Published with the financial support of the Books Council of Wales
British Library Cataloguing in Publication Data
A cataloguing record for this book is available from the British Library.
Printed on FSC accredited paper.

 Co-funded by the
Creative Europe Programme
of the European Union
 LITERATURE ACROSS FRONTIERS
 Ulysses' Shelter
PARTHIAN

This anthology is published in cooperation with Literature Across Frontiers as part of the Ulysses' Shelter project of exchange residencies co-financed by the Creative Europe Programme of the European Union. Views and opinions expressed are however those of the author/s only and do not necessarily reflect those of the European Union or the European Education and Culture Executive Agency. Neither the European Union nor the granting authority can be held responsible for them.

Contents

CONTENTS

CONTENTS

CONTENTS

Introduction

It all started on Ulysses' island

Ulysses' Cat brings readers the work of some of the most outstanding authors of the younger generation from Croatia, Greece, Serbia, Slovenia and Wales. The thirty writers and literary translators participated in Ulysses' Shelter, a project of exchange residencies originally launched by the publisher, literary agent and organiser Ivan Sršen on the Croatian island of Mljet. There, according to legend, Homer's shipwrecked hero found refuge (and was held captive for the best part of his ten-year journey home by the nymph Calypso). And this is how the idea of a project of exchange literary residencies was born, with the aim to provide 'shelter' (minus the element of captivity) for emerging writers and literary translators to spend time away from home in another country. What makes the programme particularly valuable, as opposed to the many residential opportunities for writers across Europe, is its capacity for connecting literary scenes in the participating countries and growing a network of writers who are in the initial stages of their careers.

That, in any case, was the plan when the second cycle of the programme involving five countries – Croatia, Greece, Serbia, Slovenia and Wales – started. However, the project soon faced obstacles when the Covid-19 pandemic made travel impossible, adding a new theme to contemplate and write about, that of 'isolation'. The pandemic certainly brought into focus the importance of personal, face-to-face contact and gave us new perspectives on the value of physical proximity and the thrill of meeting live audiences, in short, on everything we had previously taken for granted. While the digital had already extended the repertoire of options for contact and opened up possibilities for creative collaborations and audience reach, it now became the new normal, a levelling force that cancelled distances and made geographical and cultural peripheries equal to centres. Authors who would not have met if the project had run to plan, were brought together through digital meetings and one-to-one online discussions. Others focused on their environment, given the constraints imposed by the pandemic and the forced changes to plans and circumstances, both personal and creative.

An anthology without a theme?

There is a myriad of ways to focus anthologies: geographically, generationally, thematically. The present anthology may appear not to have a theme beyond the fact that the authors included in it belong to the same project and share perhaps nothing else than a desire to step outside their cultural environments and comfort zones. And since the reference to Ulysses, apart from being a broadly literary one, is a reference to a journey, the writers have become travel companions inside a book, who meet and take turns to tell a story.

Each also represents a literary scene, making the anthology a sampler of contemporary writing by a younger generation of Europeans with multiple referential anchors, stylistic and thematic. The majority of the texts included here, however, have not emerged from the project but have been selected from recent work already published in the original language and translated into English, which is presented, in many cases for the first time, in a book intended for the English-language market that stretches well past the borders of countries whose official language it is. Being the indisputable European lingua franca, English is sometimes seen as threatening less-widely spoken languages, and indeed several contributions to the anthology were written directly in English. Yet, the usefulness of a common language is something made clear time and again in cross-border projects whose participants, as was the case with Ulysses' Shelter, display an impressive command of English in addition to other languages, proving the point that a shared language, whatever it may be, does not diminish multilingualism, on the contrary, it confirms it, making communication possible across the continent and beyond with nuances that enrich rather than impoverish native languages.

Gazing east towards Europe

From the perspective of the Welsh literary scene, the anthology creates a symbolic bridge between Europe and Wales as a culturally and linguistically distinct part of the United Kingdom, a country that has, in the past six years been struggling with the decision to 'leave Europe' having set out on a disputed and much discussed ideological journey marked by internal culture wars. And it has been amidst the irreconcilable differences that the majority of young people and artists stand on the side of examining the roots of that decision by casting a critical glance at the country's colonial history, external and internal, and exploring what contributes to their sense of belonging.

And so, as Britain becomes metaphorically unmoored and drifts away from Europe, keeping connected through reading and dialogue provides us with new perspectives on our own changing place in the world and on the tumultuous times we live in. The works of poetry, prose and non-fiction included here offer a snapshot of the concerns and preoccupations shared by young writers from a region with a rich literature that rarely reaches English-language readers and at the same time confirm the vitality of the bilingual Welsh literary scene.

Ulysses' Cat?

And what about the cat, where does she fit in? Didn't Ulysses have a dog, the dependable Argus, who faithfully waited for him and was the only one to recognise him when he returned? And isn't the emblem of the project a donkey, the symbol of Mljet island where it represents the traditional means of transport, conveying enchantment with an idyllic past, simple, slow life, and solitude in the midst of nature without modern amenities?

But the literary references of the project span millennia: from the original, mythical Ulysses to his modernist namesake whose journey takes a day while its description fills several hundreds of pages. There, in the section named after Calypso, the nymph who held Ulysses in captivity, Leopold Bloom converses with his cat whose purring pronouncements – 'Mkgnao, Mrkgnao, Gurrh!' – become part of the meticulously detailed record of the day's minutiae and merge with Molly's sleepy 'Mn'. And aren't cats, after all, more so than donkeys, the mascots of the Mediterranean where Ulysses' journey took place? The title then is as playfully random as it is fitting: Ulysses' cat is a phantom, a conjecture, a proposition, an invitation to fabulize, to depart from well-trodden paths and imagine new stories, one of which could well begin on a light-bleached stone stage against an intense blue sea.

Alexandra Büchler

4

CROATIA

Marija Andrijašević

My sister Kamila

If I get lost I'll send you a location pin, so you can come and rescue me, he explains as he packs for Velebit. Or send help, whatever's easier. Don't worry, mountains are not so cruel in spring. It is his first hike since we've been together, and my guts are slowly crumbling in preparation for mourning at his funeral or, worse, standing in some back row because his family doesn't consider me relevant. They haven't met me yet, and we've only been together three weeks. Love is crazy, too crazy. But also short. And short loves are uncountable. Even in contemporary times, this is love's greatest drawback. Although our love has other drawbacks, more serious ones. It won't be me coming, but someone from the rescue services, You'll just have to stand quietly and wait, I think, perhaps I say it too, I definitively believe it would be just like that.

I also believe that with him I would, with time, become a rock climbing, hiking and even mountaineering enthusiast. I prepare, on the outside, carried away by his desire and yearning, note down everything I find in the pamphlets, the newsletter. My glutes will evolve from girly shapes into sporty muscles, thanks to gym machines, running schools, nordic walking, and climbing halls practice. We would always be one step behind the other, walking alongside each other, avoiding crevasses. We would stand proudly above them, literally and figuratively. Our fucking in the outdoors would not melt a glacier nor would it set off an avalanche, but it

7

would mark a comma, and possibly a colon in climate change. And from the world's peaks, drunk on passion and tired from the walking, we would sift through the clouds for lightning bolts and throw them upon the earth. I believe all kinds of things. Including the fact that our love counts, and worse – that it is love.

He cannot focus on work. He can't stop thinking about me. Today was the first time, in the seven years he's been working there, that he wanked off in the toilet. And not just in any toilet. In the boss' toilet. The boss is away on a work trip. He didn't want to take any risks. He took pictures of me at the lakes on the Savica (my trial trip to the countryside outside Zagreb) and put one of them as a screen saver on his work desktop computer. He is showing off. Domesticating me. On his breaks, and he works in the city centre as a project manager, he invites me for coffees, brunches, lunches, is late for meetings, runs across the square and shouts, under the clock where he leaves me, MARIZA, SAY YOU WILL NEVER FORGET ME. How will I forget you, you idiot, I'll see you tonight, as you ordered, at your place, in your bed.

He has even written a short story about me. The title is 'My sister Kamila' after my real sister Kamila. Well, it is more of a sketch. All because he is amazed by our names: Mariza and Kamila, and the little bits of information I have occasionally shared about myself. The story is in his head, he just has to write it. He'll do it for my birthday. He's a writer, and his job is just to … get away from his parents, their ideas about him, it's different from where you come from, what did you call it Prikom – or whatever.

The writer is young, good-looking, fit, with thick lips and healthy teeth, and lives in the attic of an Art Nouveau building, several streets away from his work. High ceilings. New windows. New paint on the walls. New wardrobes. New bed. New furniture. New floorboards. New beams. New roof. New bath. Everything feels new. New him. New me. A terrace with views of Ibler Square and the Mosque, and fountains with waves like the sea waves in Prikomurje, they awaken a melancholy in me, a feeling of familiarity. His unshaved face is lit up with the flashing lights of passing trams and seems like the most real thing I've ever seen. Mariza, what have you ever done to deserve such a bloke? You've sailed into the most beautiful bay. Careful that it doesn't turn into a tourist attraction, you've seen how all of the most attractive bays ended up on the island. Our kind wants them, but we never drop anchor in them. Quiet, Kamila, shut your gob!

I am in love, I am, I tell everyone, or rather my sister and a work colleague while we shelve books and collect magazines and I move chairs and tables with my knees in our small reading room. It's the guy that borrows four books every Monday and reads two poetry collections while browsing the shelves. You know him, I'll point him out. Ah, I sigh from the sofa, enchanted, reminiscing about his blue eyes, long fingers, big smile, he hasn't yet introduced me to his friends, but he will, just wait until we are really solid, I assure my colleague and myself. We've been together for two months now. It'll happen any time now. And the parents.

The books are always on his bedside table, neatly placed, whenever I go around, they're always in the same spot. Do you actually read them, I open one, the pages are stuck together, I rub the edges of the cover on my naked breasts. I do, of course, what do you know what I do when I'm alone. But when is he alone? Ever since he met me he keeps ringing me, wants me all the time, we have been, without a fault, glued together from the start. I'm comfortable. I have got away from the island for the first time since finishing university and spending some years back home. I have no friends or responsibilities here. But he ... He cancels birthdays, concerts, barbecues, parties. I am convinced that if I don't act in the same way eventually, he will get mortally offended. One night he cannot get an erection. He stuffs me like a turkey. It's sickening.

It's also sickening two days later, when he doesn't get in touch and it's the first time this has happened since we met. I'm worried. Maybe he's writing. Maybe he lives like a writer. I can understand that, I console myself. He might be working on Kamila. I'm suspicious of the fact that he doesn't ask for more details, that even if he is writing, I've never seen him write, he only talks about writing, and those books ... Mere objects with smooth covers. Static with dust. I think about that story, as if it were mine, and it will be mine, a gift for me, but what do I do with a bad gift? I'm ashamed to be thinking of him as a bad writer. During a lonely lunch, glancing over at his office window, and thinking about the story, I sense that something is off between us. I confide in the work colleague in a roundabout way, I don't mention being stuffed like a turkey. She tells me to google 'silent treatment', that her daughter was put in her place like that by a young man she'd fallen in love with when he didn't like her openness and assertiveness, when he'd, so to speak, started feeling like he was losing his power next to her. The school counsellor said that he had learned this at home from narcissistic parents, and that this was how they regulated one another, by hurting each other. Regulating one another? We are not thermostats! But those are ... problems of immaturity. Or worse, serious pathologies. And I kept quiet! A narcissist!

It hurts. My chest hurts the most. I cannot suck air in all the way. I fall over from the pressure at the gym, send him a message from the changing room. If I had googled what my colleague had suggested, I told myself later, who knows, perhaps I'd have sensed it in time, perhaps I'd have known not to send the message, not to apologise that evening in a bar, in public, for a simple comment about reading books, not to keep quiet when threatened with breaking up because I doubted him, that I was being too demanding and that why, oh why, can't he find a person who for once wouldn't question his words. I am not questioning your words, I sit silently, I am questioning what you do not do. And perhaps I'm wrong, he's my first city boyfriend, maybe he's right, we find it easier in Prikomurje to ... handle everything that happens to us, we are toughened from a young age, by a mother who always keeps silent and a father who instead of wrinkles has scars from fishing nets and dynamite. I keep quiet, I don't mention being stuffed like a turkey, he gives me another chance, and finally my lungs can draw in air again. I am loved!

It's a month to my birthday. The story is still a sketch. I don't ask about it, and he withdraws from me. Something is growing between us, and it isn't love. My glutes are rock hard. I'm embarrassed to have such tight buttocks because they draw looks away from newspapers, trams, posters, the road. In Prikomurje old women would cross themselves, and young men would stick their tongues under their teeth for a wolf whistle until their trousers were bulging with desire that had nowhere to go. My work colleague notices it too, teaches me how to wear my shorts twisted at the hips. Ooh-la-la. Enjoy the looks, you're young. I think of the boys on the island, I have made all of their wishes come true. I'm no longer embarrassed. The writer takes me to our first and last climb together and introduces me to his closest friends: two work colleagues and a childhood friend. I walk past the friend in the mountaineering shelter toilets and recognise the look in his eyes as the same one that hunts me down the city's streets. The writer recognises it too. Recognises desire in me, a danger. That night he fucks me with his fingers and murmurs something to himself, I know he just wants me to come. His eyes are not hungry, they're full of contempt for a woman experiencing pleasure. I've seen it in the eyes on our island, in the men who cannot be with women whose languages they don't understand, or their freedom. His hand shakes. He's tired.

We will talk about it the first chance we get, in the morning, or in two days, or five, when he gets in touch, he's spiralling again, uncatchable. This time I am not embarrassed of the thought that he isn't writing. I am embarrassed to be waiting, patiently, for him to send me a location. In his head, for a while now, I am not associated with love but with rescue. I am sad, and the sadness turns into rage. Like when mother scrubs the kitchen floor and breaks the mop, grinds her teeth at funerals, breaks rosaries in half, when she scrubs Kamila and me raw in the bath after olive harvest, so that our pale autumn skin turns red again, like in the summer. I suffer. I want something good for myself in this city. I work at the library and pound the keyboard. I start with the title, I whack the keys. My sister Kamila. Double space. Words, come on in.

He opens the door of his apartment, and a bottle of wine. I open up my heart. We open the subject of his impotence like Pandora's box, all kinds of wonders leap out of it and I am in their first line of attack. I tremble, blame myself for not having extra body parts that could replace the ones that have become insufficient. It's a long list – the scroll reaches all the way to the fountain. He cries in my lap. His vulnerability makes me comfort him like a baby. He tells me about his parents, they never let him out of sight, and when he almost lost his way whilst choosing a university degree, they quickly brought him back on track with many colourful goods. He tells me that a couple of years earlier, when two of his acquaintances published their novels (and they were good books, and popular at the library, I remember) and he graduated from the private university, he suffered something like a nervous breakdown. His parents gave him pills that they were taking for their own insomnia and psychosis, and then they took him to expensive treatment centres. What kind of parenting is that, I think, I don't want them near me. Poor him. He went to therapy once, and in forty-five minutes, more or less, he'd worked everything out. He's fine, he just has to get rid of this hatred that he feels for everyone, and everything will be great. I just want to write, he repeats. I'm sorry, I empathise, and he pulls away from me, collects himself, wipes his tears, says, what for, I am fine. Look, he doesn't say it meanly but with ease, as if he's on familiar ground, the only time I can't get a hard-on is when I'm with you. I masturbate regularly. I am healthy. Let's talk about something else. He asks me what I want for my birthday. A story. What story? The one you'd promised. A story? For you? Yes, I say self-righteously and in my local accent. What, you're pretending you forgot?

Everything hurts and I am not well. I annoy him, he hasn't been writing since he's been with me, doesn't see his friends, he's not doing his job properly, he has no problems with fucking, the problem is when the two of us have to have hanky-panky (that's what he calls it), and he unwittingly admits it has happened before, but it was never this bad, he needs more time alone, to feel the flow of ideas, to feel the PROCESS, to rest, to breathe, alone, silence,

silence. I am surprised by everything he says. We're supposed to go on a hike tomorrow. No, no, you don't get it Mariza, he's dumping you. I gather my things into my rucksack, put my trainers on. I sneak out so I don't disturb his silence. I walk to the tram station. He hates me, the thought haunts me through a sleepless night, and what could I have said or done but leave. Maybe, maybe there was something I could have done … He doesn't change his mind, there is no message. I open Facebook in the evening and find a dozen mountaineering photos. He holds his hands up in the air on the peak. It looks as if he's holding up the clouds, having shot the lightning bolt at my heart. He has a big smile on his face. He's replied to every comment since 3 pm. It's hardly been half a day, and he's already living a new life. After midnight, as soon as the app sends a notification of a wrapped-gift icon, I get my first birthday wish. Not from him.

What is this, my sister asks, who has taken an early boat from Prikomurje to the mainland, to help me. Arrange sick leave, shut the windows, tuck me into bed, wash the dishes, cook anything soupy that would start washing the guilt out of the body. I feel bad. The pain is inside my skeleton, I wobble, I cannot support itself, I fall. It's nothing compared to the pain I've inflicted on the writer, imagine what I've done, how am I going to get through this. I feel bad, why am I like this? What is this, Kamila says again and looks at the story with her name in the title. You're writing again, she asks and looks through the corrected, rewritten story. Oh it's nothing, I mumble.

Kamila heals me with stories from Prikomurje. A rich returnee from the US – whose five-floor house stuck out like a fortress among our low stone houses – has died. Everyone who has money should have the right to live forever, that's what his wife told her at the funeral.

Imagine! Afterwards the wife wouldn't speak to us, she went inside the house and demonstratively turned off the terrace lights. It was the first time we could see the stars since they built the house. I start to feel better.

No, no, he hasn't come, my colleague tells me, check the computer. True, the last thing he borrowed was returned exactly three weeks ago, on the first day of my sick leave, he's borrowed nothing since. I arrange with her that I would hide behind the shelves or in the toilets in case he turns up. At lunchtime, I manage to free myself from the terror that grips me at the desk. I don't go towards his office, nor do I look that way, I go up to Tkalčićeva this time, to get lunch, and wander around it to Opatovina. I sit on a bench with a plastic bowl full of hot stew. I don't enjoy it. I remember how I used to cook lentils, oats, buckwheat for the writer, so that he had enough to last him the week, so he didn't have to worry about food, so that he could write. I miss him and I am ashamed of the thought. I pull out my phone. I make a note on it for Kamila.

How I agreed to this, I don't know. The nordic walking group is climbing Bikčević peak on Medvednica mountain and I drag myself behind them. As I hike, I feel pain in every muscle up to my shoulder blades. I still haven't fully recovered. The flu, I tell those who ask me what's wrong, why I keep stopping. Aha, that's why you stopped coming. Take it easy. The nordic group gets in the queue for food, for seats, some are already eating by the time I reach the shelter. Mariza, Mariza, they call out to me, and I cut to the front of the queue uncomfortably. Right in front of the writer who after a brief and awkward exchange, our nodes throbbing all the way from the neck to the stomach, embraces me. It's familiar, intimate, I feel our hearts beat together, they don't resist, they surrender.

The writer is lovely. The writer is the best. Fucks. Cooks. Calls me every day. Worries about how I am. He wants us to conquer the entire city in the week that we've been back together. We trample across Zagreb like Prikomurje children stamp on grape must. I am naive and tell him that what we have now is all I ever really want. I am, again, loved! The writer doesn't want to be a writer anymore. The writer has spoken to his parents and wants a better job. The writer wants to become a leader of something, branch something out. He gets through several rounds of job interviews. He's stressed. Every conversation we have quickly ends up on the topic of his CV, job applications, what he can do, who he can talk to, the panic of whether he'd get the job, the fact that he's the best candidate, the anxiety he feels. He asks what I think about it. I am cautious. I am afraid of him.

I am afraid each time I have to say what I think, I'm afraid to think. It makes me dizzy and gives me headaches. When I talk to him I merely glance at him. I say he should do what he thinks is best. That he could save some money with a well-paid job, take some time, take a break, and write. Imagine, if I had that money, I'd write too. Have I told you about it? That in Prikomurje I have dozens of notebooks full of stories, traditions, obituaries, travel writing describing each one of the island bays. I don't need money to write, he doesn't listen to me. To write I need ... Who cares, he waves his hand. The proposed work contract is incredible, that night we celebrate with splashes of the fountain on Ibler Square and I feel like I've done a good job.

Three days. After that he doesn't get in touch for a full three days and I feel weak again. Sick. Dizzy. I am disoriented. Everything is a blur, I listen out for the sound signal at the traffic lights, rather than looking at the colours. I feel bad. What did I say? What did I do? I hold on to the shelves, doorknobs, look for an empty seat on the tram. Mariza, you silly head, you're not his girlfriend, you're his mother, washing, cooking, comforting, that's why he can't get a hard-on. Hate, hate, he doesn't hate you, he hates his own weakness, that he's not his own person, that he's not alive, and that it's clear to see. He hates that you're not stupid and so he's making you stupid. You're better than him at everything, you know? And you do it all alone. As soon as he sees you doing things, he's repelled at himself. That's why the hydraulics are out of order. He knows very well who he is and what he is. He's a fake, electric light that makes even the brightest stars fade from view. Don't go back there, you hear me? Promise! Oh, how I have betrayed you, Kamila. How I've betrayed myself, for God's sake. The writer calls, and I am flooded with fear. I don't answer. I read about the silent treatment. My head clears. I look at the colours on the traffic lights to get home.

I, Mariza Palaversa, am not loved. I am a fool who has been offered on-and-off love, and now I'm supposed to be on an off break. And what kind of love is that, I ask the writer as we take a walk around town on our break. Love with an open door, he explains and I get distracted. I think that he's a bad writer. That his analogy rests on bad foundations, a cliche. That our love rests on something similar, something feeble. I don't want a break, I want love, I say fervently, enchanted. I want passion, fire, one setting the other alight as soon as we touch! You know I'm writing a love story? In it, the heroine falls in love with a writer who doesn't write, and then she starts writing instead of him, just like she's been doing everything for him the whole time they've been together. And then, wait, hang on, let me finish, she, hey, she realises ... that she doesn't ... she doesn't love him the way a woman should love a man ... wait, you haven't heard the end, she realises that she loves him the way a mother loves her child!

It's summertime. The libraries are only open in the mornings, half of the staff are on holidays. In our bay the sea urchins are pulling back from the swimmers. Old women cross themselves, young men cross their legs. Prikomurje creaks with tourists. Some head for the US returnees' house straight off the ferry. She shoos them off and suffers aloud, shouts, swears, Kamila says look at the crazy old woman. Remember that thing she said? Everyone who has money should have the right to live forever, we say in unison. Imagine! It's summer. The time of the year for real uncountable love. Women's magazines shimmer under sun umbrellas, there is sun cream, mirror sunglasses, phone notifications asking for help. Look at it, lighting up the screen, I think. Who'd have thought he actually meant it. He's sitting somewhere hurt and waiting. He'll wait a long time. Mariza, why are you staring at that phone, come into the water, it's hot as hell. Just a moment, Kamila, I think, free, let my heart finish thumping ... it's starting to forget.

Translated by Vesna Marić

Katja Grcić

centering

you take a long time to find the right position,
ten, twenty years, maybe even longer.
you move in all the adjoining places;
check-mate the king and queen
but it remains forever unresolved.

you sit rather violently
as you read about Saturn and female sexuality.
your system growing ever quieter.
you keep turning up the heat on God to boiling
then you pour him out into voidable moulds.

you condense yourself relentlessly.
you can't sleep,
but at least you're in no rush to get anywhere.
you live in a verb tense
used to express a state before a state, and after a consequence.
when everyone simultaneously changes their minds,
it is pronounced as catapult, and spelled as
a metamorphosis of intention.
stop waving the genitive around – in any case
we all walk around hanging off the same question
where are my slippers
or

how to love and with what
you know, I imagine it this way:
at dawn
I step, barefoot, onto the balcony,
and there, here! – a revolution:
while we slept, the world bathed itself in dew.

north node

I sit down inside the north node: it is cold, dark and long-term.
needy sentences protest in cursive –
leaning over like drunk women and finally telling the truth.
but still, paper is a miserable form – a decorative, pretty
pattern in which I imprint all sorts:
Ludwig the second, an ordained woman,
the *plié* I learned at twenty-one.
I trip over on my own terrain.
I hear petals falling off lilies.
women surrendered the dresses, but not the crown. instead of a
    sceptre,
here is a post and a heresy: do not leave yourself for a week.
we will dissolve and remake everything:
water into wine, air into foam, capricorn into cancer,
man into woman.

she arrived ... and forgot everything

she arrived ... and forgot everything:
the nail box, the hearing aid,
synthetics.
of course not for him.
a denigrated lawlessness.
high heels, semiotics, then birds.
a small land mine in language
(which you'll step on)
there'll be a boom,
bring your camera,
do a selfie.

only the verse is free

no hugs except free ones
i struggle with dialectics and it struggles with me
matija why have you lost weight
don't say it was by accident

i am a dislocated triangle that was wedged into a theorem and
    told: stay there,
we'll be back –
but they never did

I confess to almighty god
and to you, brothers:
I miss no one

but
something
somewhere
keeps silent
won't say

I am earth, I need air

oxymoron

a forest, where there was once a sea.
a park, where there was once a graveyard.
what are we walled in by, do flowers sprout from it?
between flora and fauna
I never know which is which.
whenever I dream of you something spills.
after eating meat, I pick my teeth with a knife (that's what my
    ancestors did).
I invoke the words that everyone understands
and which have the strongest emotional power:
love, family, fabric.
I know nothing about the pentagram in the baptistry.
when children lie, it means that they are afraid.
when adults lie, it means that they are afraid.
I like to believe that I am wiser than yesterday
and that I know more.
an oxymoron, it is summer holidays in winter.

chrysanthemum

he says chrysanthemum
and I'm immediately over him.

she makes an event out of chauvinism:
always invites all her friends.

I was someone once, but no more.

you've bloomed with Simone, but you've no fragrance.

Petra, you're a rock and out of that rock I will build
a children's nursery, a hospital and a bird house.

to be kind all the time?
no, thank you.
and for you?
still no, thank you.
no, thank you.

the subject of the poem is her period.

if anyone asks,
I'll say chrysanthemum.

Ophelia fell off her bicycle

Ophelia fell off her bicycle and
the asphalt wove itself into her face.
five roman emperors swore on goodness.
one blade of grass wished to be a stone.

one stone finally flew, wingless
and unaware of the sinister act.
blood is warm only when it's fresh.
the soul is a butterfly in a national park,
protected, and unaware of it.
when you come, you bring me gifts.
the cloud is empty, the ground cracks under the pilgrims' feet.
the spot where we part is sacred.

irrational women and numbers

letting things go to the devil and come back crestfallen and
    unstable,
waiting for him to: translate Faust, dig up the remaining iron,
    found a city.
grow hair in the meantime and wrap it around the world like a
    noose,
be the menacing softness of blue, a sad woman with swollen
    breasts.
learn about literary devices:
avoid envy, malice, acridity and alliteration,
almost fuck up on each of those points.

agree to a thousand half solutions until one appears to be walking
　　on water.
fear a bicycle or a bin like a rescue dog,
rest on the floor, in corpse position, halfway from death by
　　hanging (everyone changes their mind at the point of no
　　return)
I am losing my talent for erotica, I become scoliosis in a porn
　　movie,
I bring sadness to where it has no place or time,
people don't add me, they mostly subtract me, you're too
　　multiplied they say,
you come like the Pi with those uncountable decimals,
no one can handle that at the moment,
we have problems at the office, you in the mind.
I miss the sea (you never change your mind in the sea)

sister:

she turned up in a strange shape and quite late.
mother was already over sixty.
but still, here she was, a sister.
she was everything I had as they say dreamed of.
beautiful, soft, with thick curly hair, ready to play.
so we played:
she put
her hand in my hair
her tongue in my mouth
her finger in my cornea
and said:

rule number one: address me as he
rule number two: be what I imagine
rule number three: surrender
rule number four: don't touch my breasts
rule number five: fuck off
desire – oxidised iron.
another's theory, a strict and tragic mistake.
I get out full of water, lungs full of water,
I take myself home, weak.
mother says:
what happened? isn't this the sister you've longed for? eh? what now?
    you don't like it?
there's no pleasing you ...
I pretend not to hear
I sit for days on a rock pulling an arrow from my neck:
if I am a deer, I'll bleed to death
if I am the sky, I'll go pink
if I am a woman, (   ) where should I go?

distance

you're an empty spot in my secondary literature
an uneven equation for the new century
an irretrievable touch

if there is a system that can envelop you
may it be gentle and imprecise
if there is a weapon that can protect you
may it be cold and in another's hand

if there is a love that will not maim you
may it be given to you each day

this is a new forest
and we are lost in it again

Translated by Vesna Marić

Maja Klarić

Ilha do Medo[1]

Today the tide is so low
That the Island of Fear is no longer an island
But something very close
And the coral reef around Itaparica
Thwarts every chance of escape
Today we are forced to stay on the shore
And face everything we have postponed

Half-written stanzas
Empty subjects
Enjambments we have used
Only to escape
From one verse to another
Buying time
And delaying the end.

Polyphony

All of those voices are mine
And none of them are
I am the sum of voices that have spoken through me

---

[1] Ilha do Medo, the Island of Fear, a miniature island in the Bay of All Saints.

And whatever was left after cancelling each other out
The difference remaining between the true stories and those I
    made up
The essence of which is my essence as well
Where all I want to say begins
Before it becomes
What it's supposed to be.

Arrival

The calm, the islands, the rain
The islands, the rain, the wind
The wind, the calm

The silence is so palpable you can hear it
And I miss everything already
Though I haven't yet arrived.

Process

The tempting part is
The overflow of ideas in the most inappropriate place
Words that could easily be transformed into sentences
An oceanic landscape, a colourful sunset, the odd passer-by
Extraordinary sights, inarticulate noises
A rare ritual secretly performed on a summer's night
The first bite of local food

An early-morning attempt to speak a foreign language at the
    market
Buying shrimps or something equally unpronounceable
Curious legends, tinged with magic
Even the local newspaper's back page
The possibility of an encounter
Of a friendship, of love
Phone calls from home
Parents' voices
A poorly lit street on your way back
The kind we promised to avoid
A pleasant stroll
An unexpected rain shower
A curious conversation
The easy part.

Shores of pleasure

In the morning
The surface of the ocean recedes inconspicuously
Like the dance of Iemanjá[2]
Summoning us to follow it
The ocean is a living room
Where older ladies sit
And idly chat
While men fish for lunch, barehanded
An unexpected current meanders in the shallow water

---

[2] Iemanjá, one of the main orixas, or gods, in candomblé, an Afro-Brazilian re-
ligious cult, the protector of the sea and fertility.

Leaving curves in the sand
Before it vanishes in the deep
And we

In a dreamlike indulgence of the first week on the island
Still incapable of believing
That nature has been so generous
To these shores of pleasure
To us.

Engaged literature

On one side of the Avenue Sete de Settembro
In the tiny antique shop Praia dos Livros
A poetry evening is running late.
By the table in the corner
A young poet from Salvador
Proudly talks of life,
The city, the people, the street,
These important topics that encompass everything
But mean nothing at all.
Half an hour later
The audience laughs with the verses
Applauds and cheers at the most interesting parts
While I am completely confused.
A discussion about literature follows
About how important it is to discuss literature
About poetry, the influence of European authors on Brazilian
    ones

Impressive conclusions, important for the future generations
Who will discuss
How important it is to discuss literature.
A sip of Saint Helena costs eight reals
And goes down much easier without looking at the Avenue
Where eight reals can get you much more
Wine.
Dragging across the pavement, naked, no cardboard mats
The cleaners of Salvador's public areas
Mostly middle-aged men and older women
Thin as the handle of a broom.
The street reeks of urine,
Of leftovers that had gone rancid in the tropical sun.
But this is precisely where I want to be
Even though I am on the repertoire at Praia dos Livros as well
I feel fake
Up here
Sheltered from myself by what's expected of me.
Everything is hypocritical
Me and my desire to change something
But I never do
The fact that I can't change anything
And that nothing ever changes
The fact that even this poem
Will be heard at a poetry reading
With just as few visitors
When I'll be reading poems about how wonderful Brazil is
Omitting all the things that make us alike
The poets and the homeless.

Scenes of summer

The tide approaches like a lover
Testing the boundaries of politeness
Reshaping the curves in the sand
And claiming the territory

Such was our travel too.
Shy at the beginning, yet ever more insatiable
As the end drew closer

In the evening we'd go swimming
Or would jump from the pier
While the sun was leaking into the sea
Like a freshly cut wound
And crabs were hysterically searching
For something that they'd lost

Just consider
How far we are from home
Think of the distance we would have to cross
If an emergency should occur there
And how long it would take us
To forget this.

Excursions
Like a picnic on a traffic island
You improvise little excursions out of the ordinary
Just so you can feel
That reality
Can still be changed
And your life
Might take a different turn
Someday.

Shapes and lines

'Whatever you think or feel, it is still not poetry.'
Carlos Drummond de Andrade, Procura da Poesia

I want to be disturbed, alarmed, challenged
The statues are more dead than dead bodies
They tell me nothing
They mean nothing
They inspire
Nothing
The street is as ordinary as a Sunday
The same here as everywhere else

I wish to be someone else
To have to go somewhere, stay there
To be ordered, to be obliged to listen
To be defined by something
To be encouraged or enraged, to react to something

But nothing happens
It is as if nothing ever happened

I'm a bystander in each situation
A bystander of my own self
Swollen with emptiness
Dry as Sertão[3]
As I wait for the thoughts and feelings to be refined into verse

And now what
Should I go crying at the caboclo's[4] feet
Should I go asking for trouble late at night on Campo Grande[5]
With my luck
Nothing
Will happen

Reconciliation

Inner and outer voices
Continually test their strengths
As soon as a gap appears
They try to equalise
Like the temperature of air in a warm and cold room
They penetrate each other and mix

---

[3] Sertão, a very dry area in the interior of Bahia.
[4] Caboclo, a half-white, half-indigenous; or someone from continental Brazil, with dark skin and straight hair.
[5] Campo Grande, the main square in Salvador with the statue of a caboclo in the middle; there is a saying 'crying at the caboclo's feet' meaning crying or complaining in vain.

Trying to reach equilibrium
But of course they never succeed
Because with both one and the other
Something always chafes
A stone in their shoe
On a leg long-ago amputated
As an eternal surplus
An empty phrase

Amor, Ordem e Progresso[6]

To feel everything in every moment
In each place, each situation
To immerse yourself in the sand
Without fear

To feel everything in each alleyway
Each harbour, each port
To speak in all languages
To stretch like a palm tree
But to still feel the unease
For everything might as well be nothing

But nothing could also be everything

---

[6] *Ordem e progresso*, meaning 'order and progress' in Portuguese, the inscription on the contemporary Brazilian flag that used to begin with the word amor i.e. love.

Upon departure

Only during our last crossing
From Itaparica to Salvador
Somewhere in the middle of the bay
Did we realise we were leaving
That day we came to Salvador
Only to leave it
And commence another journey
That of a return

If only the trip home could be shorter
Or much, much longer
Long enough to forget
Where we departed from
And where we are going

The city assumes the face
Of the person most difficult to say goodbye to
And devastates us with its silence

It will take time before we realise
That we are the only ones who decide
Whether the world is too big
Or too small

Translated by the author

Dino Pešut

Madge

1.

The day that my beloved Madge died was the day a new neighbour moved into the building. I cried inconsolably. He didn't look as if he belonged in this part of town. He should have been living in the new centre. People often cry in front of our building. Especially in the summer. He didn't know that. He stood beside me and with a heavy accent, and bad grammar, asked me if I was feeling all right. I showed him the dead Madge.

Then Hans arrived with two beers. But it was Hans who needed the beers more than me, because Hans is a proper alcoholic. I just needed to calm down.

2.

My new neighbour ties up his bicycle to the tree under my balcony. I greet him every day. He has a pink bike. I think he's gay. And this is a gay neighbourhood. I am often on the balcony. Especially since Madge died. It's more pleasant and I can greet the neighbours. I don't have many guests at the moment, but there'll be lots in the next few weeks. I have tried to invite the new neighbour for tea or a glass of wine, but he is always in a hurry. And he always says 'next time'. I have plenty of time now. While Madge was alive, I didn't have so much time. She was old and sick and I always needed to take her to the doctor. It was also expensive. It's not a nice thing to say, but since Madge died I have more time and money. Which also means I could have a new boyfriend.

3.

My new neighbour – I have since found out what his name is, but I want to protect his identity – has not been home for a few days now. I mean, I didn't worry much at first. In this city, people often don't come home. It was also the weekend. They meet someone and disappear for a few days. It's normal. Especially if they're young and good-looking, like my new neighbour. It's easy to meet people that easily in this city. But you need to be careful. The clinic in our building is constantly active. And all those boys who cry in front of our building learn that there are consequences. But it's been five days now, and I haven't seen the bicycle. I'm really worried that something has happened to him. I miss Madge. The guests arrive tomorrow.

4.

When I have guests, then I can spend less time on the balcony. Especially when the naturists come. Considering the fact that the flat is on the ground floor, we have to keep all the curtains closed. Every now and then I peek through the window and I see my neighbour leave and I know he won't be back until the morning. He probably has a boyfriend or several boyfriends. This kind of thing is not unusual in this city. When I have a lot of work with the guests, then I worry about Hans because he's very lonely. He has lost his job again and I know he's drinking a lot now. And I prefer it if he drinks with me because then I know how much he's had to drink. And when he gets really drunk, he can sleep on my sofa. My Madge would then lie next to him to console him a bit. When I stop being so busy with the guests, I will have to dedicate myself to Hans.

5.

I have had guests all the time. And I have to look after everything which means that I haven't had the chance to pay attention to the new neighbour. This flat is very small, but there is really a lot to do. And I have to be the perfect host. I have to keep an eye on the wine because I can't relax. I'm saving for a new sofa. Some guests complained the sofa was uncomfortable and I had to offer them my own bed. While Madge was alive, she would entertain the guests while I worked. But now I have to do everything. I have to entertain them, I have to clean, I have to do everything. It's not easy. And it's a lot of work. So I don't have time to take care of my love life. And that's not good. If only Madge was still alive, things would be so much easier. Everyone loved her. Maybe the neighbour would have come for a visit if she was still alive. I invite him every time, and every time he says 'next time, I'm in a hurry now'. No one is ever in a hurry in this city.

6.

My new neighbour has had a bit of a haircut and he looks great. But he's also put a bit of weight on, which doesn't make him look so great.

7.

There are good and bad days. Today is a bad day. I think I ate something that was off. I don't know what happened. I'm vomiting. Maybe it was the wine. Hans said it was good wine. For cooking and for drinking, plus cheap. But what does Hans know? Hans is a real alcoholic. I don't feel well. And it's hot. It's not a good day. I don't need to say that I miss Madge. She would lie next to me now and everything would be better. Just a bit better. How nice it would be if my new neighbour would lie next to me. I believe in destiny. I believe that Madge's spirit has entered my new neighbour. Such coincidences simply don't happen.

8.

My neighbour is crying under my balcony. That's never a good sign. I hope he isn't sick. I ask him if he's all right in perfect German. He answers in English:

—No, they stole my bicycle.

I know it's not nice, especially in this neighbourhood, to say that I was relieved. I invited him over for a cup of tea or a glass of wine. And this time he accepted. Men are particularly beautiful when they cry. Luckily, the flat was tidy. I showed him everything.

My wall dedicated to Madonna. All the tickets to her concerts. From my youth. I showed him the DVD of the film I acted in. We even watched the scene I was in. 42:53. He said I was really authentic. I showed him a photo of Hans. And said, in confidence, that he was a real alcoholic. He keeps losing his jobs because of boozing. I offered him wine. Not Hans's wine, but a better one. He said it was too early for him, but it was past noon. I did a stupid thing and had a glass of wine. But before that I'd had a beer and I belched loudly. He pretended not to hear.

He asked about Madge, and I showed him her ashes.

He couldn't stay long. He said he had a lot of work to do. In the end he smiled. He has beautiful teeth, even though he smokes. I'd like to have all my teeth.

9.

Today my new neighbour and I arranged a funeral. I finally buried Madge. It was time, and he buried the chain of his bicycle under the tree outside our building. It was sad. Next to us two young men cried, but not because of the bicycle or Madge.

– It's time to go on – he said. His German wasn't getting any better. I have accepted that I am not his type. And that we'd never be together. That's just how it is in life. He probably likes boys that are bigger and younger than me. This is normal for the young. And he definitely has someone in the new centre of town. I am too busy with guests anyway and I'm thinking of going back to acting. And I don't have time for a new boyfriend anyway. I think it's time to dedicate my time to myself. And he needs his space. His flat upstairs is really dirty. And he said he can't stay there anymore. And I've come to terms with the fact that one loses people really easily in this city. Some give up, and some, whom I once knew, die.

10.

Today something truly awful happened. Early in the morning, before ten, there was shouting under the balcony. I recognised my neighbour's voice. I ran out, even though I wasn't looking my best. He ordered me to call an ambulance. He was squatting next to a man who was prostrate under a tree. He was trying to turn him on his side. This is a common sight in the inner yard of our building. It's dark and people overdose or faint or whatever. I thought that my neighbour shouldn't be touching that man. You never know.

– I think this is your friend Hans! – my new neighbour shouted. This was the first grammatically accurate sentence he had uttered. And really, I recognised Hans' favourite T-shirt. I wasn't quite all together because I was still sleepy. I'd had a bit of that rancid wine before going to bed again. I couldn't remember the emergency number. I ran upstairs to the clinic and shouted that we needed a doctor. They thought I was some crazy person. People often don't trust me if I haven't tidied myself up. But when the doctor looked through the window and saw the neighbour and Hans, he ran down the stairs.

I was glad that there was nothing wrong with Hans, except that he was drunk again. I was not glad that the handsome doctor and the new neighbour started flirting. You can tell straight away. We put

Hans on my sofa and he was put on a drip.
I cancelled all my guests for the next two weeks.

11.
The day my new neighbour moved out of the building, I got myself
a new cat. I got it more for Hans than for myself. He really needed
it. We called it Madge, because we decided that that was the best
name for a cat.

Translated by Vesna Marić

Maja Ručević

High-rise phantoms

Ferid is forty-four. Unmarried. Unemployed. Lives with his mother. Barely finished high school. For three years after that, he spent every night drinking in bars, and then the war came. He avoided the war with the excuse of poor eyesight requiring a strong prescription. Now he avoids life with the excuse of the war that took away his best years and the ones that followed. He doesn't have any applicable and useful knowledge or skills. He lives in a country where people pray in four different types of temples, steal and cheat in every season of the year and crawl on all fours to survive the effects of a four-year long 'conflict which includes organised use of weapons and physical force by countries or other social groups' – this was a definition of war he found in Wikipedia. After his first breakdown his mother declared that it wouldn't have come to that if he had studied more and fooled around less. After the latest one, she took him to a hodja to hear some readings from the holy book but before they even started, the Quran moved by itself and the potential saviour quickly sent them home without the promised healing. He doesn't know the first thing about love. The most complicated relationship he's had with a woman was a one-night stand. He gave it a chance three or four times. A hooker he picked up in a no-name village where he used to buy weed told him his cock was definitely bigger than his IQ. He stuffed her mouth with it. That was also his last 'intimate encounter' with a woman. After his father died, he told his mother he would eventually leave the country. She told him

44

if that happened, her heart would break with sadness. As they said this to each other, a grenade fell on the house next door, killing his uncle. Mother's heart broke with sadness. Ferid went to the funeral. Shovelling the soil of the land he would never leave, he contemplated suicide. He has one acquaintance, Ejub Stevica. E. S. is one of those people who are happy to do anything unrelated to earning a living. He believes that it is perfectly enough for a person just to stare at the TV day after day. Ferid stares with him, day in, day out. They mostly watch *Animal Planet*. At night, Ferid dreams of slimy male frogs who grip eggs with impressive leg skills, and drag them to a damp place to bring a next generation of tadpoles to life. He also dreams of Ejub Stevica. A lot. The two of them falling in some kind of an abyss. When he's alone he sometimes thinks about things happening around him. Whether, for whom, and why it all matters. This minute or two of brain activity tires him out soon and then he goes to the kitchen to eat, then he shits, smokes, pisses, coughs, moves around the house or the street, aimlessly, with no sense of time, before coming back. Before going to bed, he doesn't say goodnight to his mother, doesn't perform any ritual. He drops on the couch and snores. Once he told Ejub he didn't like his life. That he was troubled by being unsuccessful, passive, lifeless, uninteresting, ugly and not having any interests or motivation. He told him that he hated the fact he never went to the movies or for a drink with someone, that he was lonely and wished he had a girl, that he felt he would die leaving no one and nothing behind, and that maybe he would try to change things, but he didn't know where to start. Ejub just shrugged his shoulders and said he was *whacked*, called him *dude* and rolled a joint that burned away at the same speed as Ferid's nonsense talk about the possibility of a better tomorrow. One afternoon he found himself in the company of two girls Ejub brought over. The movie *Grbavica* was on TV. During a gruesome scene with the mothers of Srebrenica, Ferid commented that he would surely cry if the two of them weren't around. One of the girls said that crying is human, not reserved only for women. The other one mentioned genocide. The first one drew a connection to the Holocaust. The girls exchanged appalled looks and left shortly after. That night, Ferid admitted to himself he knew nothing. He thought he was stupid. The next day he shut himself in his room. The following couple of months he didn't leave the house, except to go to a local store to buy cigarettes. He would come down to the dining room to eat what his mother had cooked, then go back to his bed. Aunt Mina said this was called depression, he overheard her whispering it to his mother in the kitchen. Despite all of his shortcomings, Ferid knew there was one thing preventing him from failing completely, immediately and in every sense – he wasn't insensitive. He deeply felt everything that was happening to him, he just never knew how to express it. For example, he was unquestionably aware of a great amount of anxiety and discontent piling up in him over the years, but he didn't talk about it. Sometimes he even felt something resembling happiness – once he helped a faltering old man cross the road. The old man thanked him, and Ferid felt an overwhelming sense of mercy and pride. The worst thing was his sadness: essentially, he was sad all the time, he often woke up at night crying for no reason. But he couldn't say this to anyone. And there was actually no one to tell. Solitude was a mould his sadness poured into, like dough into a baking tin. One night he dreamed of his father, a man who spent most of his life gambling, drinking and beating up his mother and him. In the dream, his father appeared in the form of a *melek*, looming over him with some kind of gaudy sparkly wings, saying: 'Son, this life you are living is a dark realm. But don't let it break you. Only the honest and hardworking man will enter *Jannah*. Do something or you will disappoint both God and me.' Having said this, he flapped his grotesque wings and flew away in an unknown direction. A sunny morning dawned. The room was full of eerie silence. Once, in a TV show, Ferid heard that the French have this saying: when a moment of silence happens in a conversation, that this is because an angel is passing by. Ferid thought his entire life was like that, an angel passing by. Somewhere in the neighbourhood, a baby cried. He was gripped by a grim sense of horror. Then, when his mother called him, he asked himself why she had given him this name, which is supposed to mean unique, incomparable.

Translated by Petra Pugar

GREECE

Iakovos Anyfantakis

When he only had forty-five drachmas

I say to him gimme four hundred
What could I have said, the man was shoeless.

Thanassis Valtinos, 'Spare me fifty drachmas for cigarettes?'

His favourite story was about the time when he was left with forty-five drachmas. It wasn't a day or a period, it was a whole lifetime, the time he had spent with forty-five drachmas in his wallet. He didn't talk about it with nostalgia, nobody can be nostalgic about being poor, certainly not him, although he could be nostalgic about being young, being healthy, not having yet been through all the suffering that would come later, which was plenty even though he did artfully hide it. Still, he didn't talk about it with sadness or with fear or didacticism, there was nothing to teach others about 'when he only had forty-five drachmas'. And it wasn't a story as such. It was a sequence, a world, a universe like they say nowadays in films and comic strips, not just an era but an aggregate of characters and situations whose stories began and ended with 'when I only had forty-five drachmas'.

He talked about it with the calm and sense of distance of someone talking about a man they'd met earlier in the street: saw him from inside a car, behind glass, there had been no words exchanged but they spent quite some time observing him. It no longer meant anything that he used to live with forty-five drachmas in his wallet, though he well remembered the feeling of hunger and shame – hunger not because he was ashamed but shame because he was hungry and not only for that.

Hunger. He'd read many books about hunger – literary, medical, political – some fairly accurate and well written, some most likely based on first-hand experience, but none could satisfactorily describe what hunger was. For him, hunger was divided in three levels, the bodily hunger, that sensation that originated in the stomach, which felt vacant, aching, you could feel the blood going into it as if trying to fill it up and then, that pain dispersing throughout the body, forcefully, like small nails under the skin. Then, there was the level of despair. Poor sod, you'll never eat again, you won't make it, I'm sorry, people do die from hunger, ingloriously, and besides, hunger is not just a need, it is also a pleasure and you will never again feel the joy of bread with olive oil and feta cheese in your mouth. Third was the level of envy. Look at the people around you. Everyone, each one separately and all together, they have all eaten and will eat again, most have even wasted a little bit of their food, but not you, you will go on hungering and aching till you die.

Shame. Shame for his parents who were poor, shame for himself who remained poor, shame that he had no way of stopping being poor, shame for being ashamed and shame that he wasn't ashamed enough to do something about it. Shame when others spoke and he didn't dare speak because he had forty-five drachmas and, were the conversation to turn to money, what could he possibly say? Shame when they weren't saying anything because he had to talk and he only had forty-five drachmas. Shame when they were looking at him because they might know. Shame if they weren't looking at him, because surely they must know.

He was now talking about 'when he only had forty-five drachmas in his wallet' because these stories needed to be preserved, that man – meaning himself – ought not be forgotten, others needed to hear, some of them might be with forty-five cents in their pocket right now, that this is a real possibility, but it can come to an end twenty, thirty, fifty years later, not all that long that is, and they can find themselves with a business, a house with a garden, a country place, three apartments to rent and collect rental, two stores, a bank account, an orchard, farmland, a great deal of money in the bank and an inflatable boat five metres ninety long, with a hundred and fifty horsepower engine. He was saying it, finally, because he probably thought it was a nice, impressive story that held others' attention and, overall, he didn't have too many stories, at least not ones that others liked to hear and this was a series of stories that seemed to keep them somewhat engaged.

There was the story about when he didn't have money for a ticket and made his way back on foot. Many times. The story about the girls he didn't ask on a date because he couldn't pay, no matter where he took them. The stories of the nights when he hadn't eaten all day and was causing himself pain in order to forget the pangs of hunger. The story about when he had found some food but was afraid to eat. The story about his clothes being worn so that he could only sit in a particular way for the holes not to show and everyone thought he had a muscle spasm. The story about those shoes he really liked and – it just so happened – he could afford but, alas!, he hadn't known they were summer shoes and wore them all through the winter, even though everyone else could tell, those weren't shoes for wearing in the rain or snow, but they were the only ones he had and he would laugh it off, describe their high manufacturing standard and how he didn't believe in the cold and, so wasn't cold.

The amount was certainly odd. 45 drachmas were too few, not

even fifty, yet it wasn't altogether nothing. It was something quite specific. It was more than nothing and, at the same time, not enough for anything. There is no way that this is what he always had in his pocket, it must have been more, at times maybe less, yet all the stories, he persisted in talking about when he only had forty-five drachmas, as if that exhausted the pocket's capacity and if any more went in, they slipped back out or, as if some tiny fairy immediately replenished what he spent.

The weird thing is, he never planned to stop only having forty-five drachmas. He didn't expect to. Didn't imagine it. Yes, he'd heard of others who didn't have anything and then they did, but those were other ones, they thought differently, were shrewder, smarter, all he wanted was to live, to survive, that was more than enough, it was far from certain, to escape poverty, yes, that'd be good, something to wish for, but that was the extent of it. Nothing more. As to how it happened, it wasn't so different from anything that happened in all similar situations. Besides, as has been noted, he was neither dumb nor lazy nor a spendthrift. He had good, square common sense, he enjoyed saving, orderliness, he studied things and situations before going into action. At one point, somehow, he got hold of a thousand drachmas. Then, one thousand became two thousand. The two became four, the four eight. Strangely – and this he had neither expected nor imagined – it is easier to turn sixteen thousand to thirty-two than forty-five drachmas to one hundred. Then everything follows on a course by itself, the business we mentioned, the house with the garden, the other houses, the stores, the country place, not to go over that long list, even the inflatable with the hundred and fifty horsepower engine (and another spare one which, however, will never be needed.) But he didn't tell these stories, he thought them rather boring, arrogant, what did the other person care about the deal he got on the apartment in the square, when he rescued that fellow from being repossessed by the banks, but he also got it at cut price because he had the cash and within five years, got his money back from the rent and has had revenue ever since so that he could also buy the plot behind the main street and put up an apartment block, selling off three of the apartments straight away to pay his debt and keeping two plus the store and it's now all clean profit.

After that, there weren't any stories anymore. There was just profit. There was also a good life, not happiness, there were other reasons that this couldn't be, but, well, you see, knowing for sure that you'll be able to eat both at noon and at night, when there have been days when you were certain of the opposite, does make for a kind of joy. Knowing there's clothing for the child. Being there if your neighbour's going through a rough patch. Having on the good summer shoes in summer and the warm winter ones in winter. Not needing to mentally add up, then subtract from the month's salary, before ordering from the restaurant's menu.

The years were fine that came after. And there were many of them. So many that eventually, there was no one left of those who knew him when he only had forty-five drachmas. As he aged, though, those stories kept multiplying, some might even have been imaginary, but he pulled them out with ease, at every opportunity and forced them on his listener. Often, he didn't limit himself to one, because each story led to another and then, somehow, yet another and none of his listeners felt like disconcerting him because he really was courteous and he was modest and, mainly, because everyone knew that he'd never turn you down if you were in need. For sure, some thought he was saying those things to give them courage 'don't fret, see what I went through and where I got to, you can too, the Lord is merciful', though, after a while, most thought that maybe it was more a need of his to talk and reminisce about it all, because he missed it, because that was the one place where he felt at ease, when he only had forty-five drachmas, that's who he was, who he became afterwards never really making a dent, he was like a migrant who many years later, speaks nostalgically of his homeland, no matter that life there was dreadful, full of beatings, poverty and sickness. Which is why when he passed, after much suffering, released from a long sickness, his son thought of putting forty-five drachmas inside the pocket of his good suit, so that he could feel comfortable in his grave, or in the next world, or wherever he was off to, but there weren't any drachmas in the house anymore, and it was nigh impossible to find some at such short notice, what with all the preparations and so many people coming to pay their respects from all over, so they buried him without any and when his son thought about that in the cemetery, he cried for the first time for his poor old dad.

Translated by Konstantine Matsoukas

Filia Kanellopoulou

Background

Late at night
I will silently open the balcony door
and as I step out
the wind will lift me up high like a raven's feather
and I will become one
with the lights of your city
that had previously
in the dark
haunted my sleep

In a little while I will step on your roof tiles
I will feel with my fingers the impressive pediments
the antennas on the roofs,
the ceilings of the houses I will caress
my tears may become drops on their windows,
my face plaster relief, a façade ornament
my body – a former shooting range –
will become one with the ruins
I will turn into an attraction
holding a sceptre, a statue
or an adornment in a marble water fountain,
the second plan, that is,
a background
for photos
of your foreign visitors.

Ode to legs

My legs
strong legs, you were my support
in the most difficult
the biggest
the first step of life
you walked me in the streets of my world
known and
unknown
My legs, we ran together
on so many pavements
we danced together to all kinds of music
we travelled to cities
of the world
we climbed hills
you swam, my legs
you gave the first leg-up
you climbed with me
through doors, into libraries
up simple stairs
you rose to the challenge
and landed me on the descent
beautiful legs – as everyone is saying –
you opened at the sight of my lovers
you wrapped yourself around bodies and grasped waists
you supported me in earning my daily wage
you sat gracefully on chairs
you exercised with me and
you got a role, after that
'Do the candle pose while saying the words.'

O my feet, you!
You endured all this,
to hurt, after the journey ...
Now it makes sense!
How much more can you endure
two years inside now
all numb?

With the paper

I hold the pen with one hand
and as I am about
to grab the notebook with the other,
– to write something about you –
I cut my finger with the paper
I stand and look at the blood
coming out of the small hole
and I don't understand
is it an omen, a sign not to write this poem
I put down the pen
and write with blood
only then can I
write something about you.

Above and below the stage

After so long
I finally saw a play
in a foreign language
I wear my nice clothes
and light make-up
I don't know what they say
but I laugh out loud
and I cry at times
for Sofka's life
or for the delusions of Ilja
who believed he was being followed by spies
I understood the play from beginning to end
in all the languages of the world
People
rejoice and suffer the same
and in the same way
above and below the stage
they overcome obstacles

Infinite sequels

An amazing image in the city centre
captured my gaze and thought
In a circular square
there are four benches in a semicircle
on these benches sit four people
one on each

and everyone is talking on their phones
I wonder
what they talk about
Four people, four stories
Have they recently lost a loved one
or was a new member of the family born?
Was it a divorce
or a wedding?
Is the woman pregnant
or did she just have an abortion?
Are the men actually talking on the phone
or do they not know how to flirt with her as they surround her?
Why are these people so lonely that each one sits on a separate
    bench?
Are they afraid?
We all are afraid of others lately
But after they went into the trouble of getting out of the house
or leaving work
at least they could sit down together to share these stories
Yet instead of writing a common one, they gave in again to their
    loneliness
And you will ask me now without being entirely wrong
why is all this so interesting

that I start with the phrase 'an amazing image'
I don't know
It's that sometimes I think like a director
From this static frame
in front of us open up four
and therefore infinite
sequels

Translated by Thanos Chrysanthopoulos

Often, it's heard

Like tombs they fall upon us
our brothers, our cousins, our father and mother
News headlines, like dirt they fall upon us
Journalists, they bury us deeper and deeper
those gravediggers
Teachers dig up pits for us
Bosses drink our blood
Husbands secretly beat us
Society openly skins us
A woman neighbour talks about us as we pass by
another one asks 'When will you tie the knot?'
Colleagues want to 'rape us'
(this is something that is heard a lot in corporate offices)
Supervisors want to see us in tears
(that's what they told me once, laughing)
When they want us alive, it's only to give birth
to raise their bastard kids
for them to be able to continue
building a world in their own image

Underneath the city
In memory of Vasilis Mangos

Underneath the streets we walk
and underneath the houses we live in
run sewers
a vast network of wastewater pipes

flowing
underneath the city
in summer we swim
where sewage is dumped
we plant plastic in the forests
and breathe
right where
we burn our garbage
and if we don't want to live like this,
if we want to live differently,
the underground
collective shit
rises to the surface
to drown us
and somehow like this
we die in our sleep of 'something' called
'pulmonary oedema'
but we're to blame
having built our shared home
on an abundance of filth!

Translation by Yiannis Varvaresos

Dimitris Karakitsos

The Algerian

Daybreak. The heroes of the short story at hand have fallen asleep on the loungers. They are exhausted. I ill-treated them all night long. I didn't allow them to make love. The night was warm, I made the boy's guitar fall on the tiles of the verandah to startle them. I let loose the horse and the youths followed it, finding the door to the neighbouring house open. A television was playing at low volume, the goldfish shimmered inside the aquarium. The doors banged in the wind, an elderly man was asleep in the courtyard. He was sleeping in his rocking chair, pieces of watermelon were pooling on the plate. My heroes wanted to make love, the narrow street running between the country houses was redolent with the milky scent of fig leaves. I decided on a dramatic twist for my story. A dog (the elderly man's dog) gave chase to the youths. To save themselves, they split up: the girl leapt over the fence and hid, the boy went down a narrow path. He found himself in the courtyard of the last house and from there, through a hedge of thorny greenery, he started calling to his beloved whistling in code. The two youths got back together, used a stone to break the window pane of a mobile home and lay down on an unmade bed. They took their clothes off, kissed and embraced but the owner's sudden return, which I made up, separated them again. The man came without warning, like a gust of wind, his car lights piercing the windows. There was honking and the sound of keys at the door. Stark naked, the youths made their escape laughing, while the incensed Pekinese of the newly arrived owner frothed at the mouth with rage. The youths found refuge in the house next door and kissed again at the far corner of a rock garden. I gave a push to the swings and they started squawking, like birds scattered by a gunshot. Past 3 am, my heroes realised that it's beautiful to wander around naked under a sickle moon. No matter if you're being pursued, no matter where you might be heading, the important thing is the warm body walking alongside you. The girl ran to the beach and the boy went back to the house. He returned with clothing in his arms, then they hugged in the semi-dark. I threw pebbles in the sea. I heard their whispers. They talked about the dog that chased them, about the mobile home break-in and about it being somewhat painful sprinting with an erection. I could have separated them with a swarm of mosquitoes but it was daybreak and they'd fallen asleep leaning against each other.

Now the night has been eroded, the sea has the colour of ash and the present has become the past, and this story must be forgotten before the light of day comes upon it.

The music of Enriko Zanis

The fragrant lemon trees with the bronze branches on Dousmani street endured an adolescent's slashing despite my angry shouts, despite the threats. I ran out to get him but I only found his razor in the grass. (It was an old razor with a bone handle.) The wounds on the trees formed the letter E, the shutters of the apartment block with the grey-orange awnings were banging en masse in the wind. Just then, a reflected light in my eyes blinded me. Professor Enriko Zanis was toying with a mirror. He said good morning, although it was afternoon, and welcomed me into the decrepit apartment block: a realm of silence with unkempt staircases and a dark corridor. The light fixture of the stairwell was falling apart and its ruby-coloured beams picked out a yellow rose fallen on the wooden boards. My guided tour started from the single flat (the flat I was to rent) next to the professor's apartment. But for one residence on the first floor, which was vacant and in a dismal state, the rest of them all had the same furniture and wallpaper. Let me remark that the rent my professor was asking, was suspiciously low. Before I could get an explanation, though, at the end of the semester, Enriko Zanis had a heart attack. His appearance at the counterpoint class after an appropriate amount of time, made us wonder if his place had been usurped by some quiet clone. From the chubby court jester, we were abruptly the students of a weird formalist who would start classes without any delay. I used to accompany him shopping – I remember his chequered coat that smelled of sandalwood. I remember him lifting his sleeve every so often to check the time. (One afternoon, I found a wall clock in the hallway.) I would hear Enriko Zanis talk to himself. I'd see shadows in the hallway. I would find yellowed postcards in my letterbox. I was sure Enriko Zanis was leaving them and one day I dropped them under his door. To sum up: an adolescent who was carving the lemon tree, a yellow rose, a ghost-apartment block and an inexplicable about-turn. Unconnected bits at first sight which, however, will very soon fall in place as parts of Enriko Zanis' sad obsession.

* * *

That afternoon I took a shortcut through the city alleyways, perused a bottlebrush at someone's doorstep and saw a man and wife kissing. At the entrance to the apartment block, I found a yellow rose. I knocked on Enriko Zanis' door, I noticed a violin with broken strings on top of a pile of books. The frayed bits of the wallpaper had grown mouldy and the walls had a strange sheen to them. I handed my assignment to the professor and he asked me to wait for him in the study room. He then withdrew to the kitchen to make some tea. In a picture hanging on the wall, I recognised the adolescent who had carved the lemon trees. There was the sound of the tray with the teacups crashing to the floor. Enriko Zanis was weeping, his forehead bleeding from some sharp fragment. I helped him up. He told me that everything happening at this moment is a dream I'm having and we were suddenly transported to the empty room on the first floor. A ram was there, convulsing, with its throat cut. I knew I was inside a dream and I urged Enriko Zanis to tell me the truth.

* * *

Vincenzo Papiamonis, a prehistoric legend of Corfu theatre, was slowly dying in his country home among trees and shrubs, in rooms with wall hangings, filled with paintings and candles, said Enriko Zanis. Using a walking stick for support, he would take me by the arm and we'd walk along a narrow dirt road under the shade of the pines, he wore a cardigan though it was July, a green cardigan, and spoke to me about the year before the war, the German bombings, the spectre of the explosion pouncing through the city alleyways with shards of glass and pieces of roof tiles. But all that was long gone, and the tri-fold Vincenzo never parted with (I recall his bony and, strangely, rosy fingers caressing it) was a scorched theatre programme with his name in the second row. I wondered what might there be left from that performance? My colleagues have all died, Vincenzo would say, and 'Portio', aka Aristides, all too young, in a car crash in Athens, in '29. I will let you in on my final wish: I'd like to bring them all back to life, in our costumes at the old theatre for a commemorative photo. I vaguely remember our director backstage and a dim light, whenever I lie down I leave a small light on, and I think it'd be just the same if there was some record or other, that survived from the performance: it would be an insignificant victory over the dark, but that's now impossible. The performance will pass into oblivion, once I take with me all these laughable (saying this, he chuckled) memories.

Vincenzo died shortly after, the newspaper graced him with a single column, one hundred words sketching a *favourite actor of the Interwar years*. They recalled the stooped old gentleman (leaning over his walking stick, the writer said) who always left a large tip for the waiters at the Olympia restaurant. Typical, the superficiality of the press, their eagerness to draw out big emotions. What, though, could be more tragic than the real terror, the irreversibility of oblivion? Vincenzo believed that a black-and-white snapshot could balance the past by preserving a vitality that had faded long ago: memories that only concerned himself. Still, no matter how unfeasible it all sounded, Vincenzo's idea about a victory against the darkness had begun to haunt me: the first libretto I wrote was overly ambitious. It fulfilled, in a way, the wish of my old friend: a troupe of old actors on the stage again, their legs heavy like someone wading through a swamp, confessions and elderly boastings just before the director's sudden collapse on the theatre seats.

The libretto spent a long time in my drawer, when I picked up the subject again, I determined to take ownership of it: rather than Vincenzo's performance, I tried to recreate an excursion. It had taken place fifty years ago, I was sixteen, first time in love, there were only two groups in the village we were visiting on that day in May, with a fair distance between them, yes, but not such that they couldn't hear each other's taunts. However many albums I leafed through I couldn't find a single photograph from that excursion – my siblings didn't even remember it. In short, the protagonist in the second libretto was going to be me. But all the initial attempts to write a musical score for the libretto failed. I became all fired up: initially driven by the tragic story of Vincenzo, with the conceit that I was in possession of an artistic treasure, each failure to dress the play with notes plunged me into a short-lived breakdown. All this would have gone on indefinitely if the heart trouble hadn't intervened, the first arrhythmias. As a result, the doctor's assessment (I realised things were serious) meant that the completion of my work was now a one-way street. I wanted to save myself. Many times I would write music in my sleep, or fall to the floor without a pulse. To describe it, I'll use a metaphor. Imagine a transparent book, each of its pages partakes with unyielding synchronicity in the others exiling linearity from the realm of corruption: this was my music, a timeless landscape. But then inexplicable things started to happen. You yourselves were witness to one of those: It was me who carved the lime trees that afternoon, I had returned from a time travel and the razor in my hand had been a gift from my father for my first shave. There were times when I would wake up in my armchair from songs and tales from another era and then, looking outside, I'd see the beach, my uncles dancing, an overturned boat on the sand, the yellow rose my aunt wore on her bosom. The tablecloth and our dishes with the leftovers, or my sweet dad smoking and gazing at me.

* * *

Look at me, said Enriko Zanis, I am bleeding and soon I might be no more, but you are a witness to my success: you are the living photograph that Vincenzo never got to relish. You are me and your name is Enriko Zanis!

Through my eyes, you have seen myself as an adolescent and through your eyes I will continue to live, in this house which half a century earlier took me in as a student. In a short while, with my last word another second life begins for you, same as the one I lived and which you will relive, thanks to the music we wrote: look at me was Enriko Zanis' last phrase, all through your life I will follow you.

Translated by Konstantine Matsoukas

Nikolaos Koutsodontis

Airplane travel

You were cold, on a playground bench.
With what flesh I could find in the cold
I covered you.

When you inconvenienced me on the sofa,
pouncing on my fears with your saliva,
you were a kiosk in Patission Street, on fire.

There was that night when you took my clothes off.
The room foundered
leather swam with the rug
the sports equipment and the books
sunk, a mess.

You had to leave.
Two open seas kept us apart
filled with invisible dogfish.

A decal on the mirror
and the thing went on like
a mob in a game with violence.

After the layoff

I want to eat my degree
with a Friday's Mexican Meal.
I will pay with money borrowed from my parents.

I will lend my palms to holiday home floors
so that Filipino women can scrub them
while singing hymns to The Lord.

To the man, dead inside me,
I will give a wedding ring,
washing his feet so they won't smell.

In the trolleybuses I will give my seat to the flies
respecting the free fluttering of wings.

Every moment, a darkness puts out my cigarette
I find myself in Titanic's lounge
with the sixteen-year-old bell boys
and the last boat has departed.

Boys seduce Ariadnes in the big malls
outside skating parks, with spilled coca-colas
on the city hall signs.

In my mind I weave labyrinths with snow
scary, like the ones at Overlook Hotel.

They promised me growth and indexes
in streets with African whores.

The building moved to Elaionas, with the refugees.

And from the balcony I gaze at Lycabettus
filled with twilight, in my thirties.

Ambelokipoi, in one street

To Zachos and Dimitris

We changed the wallpaper
on all our walls
to colours of our own.
Using our savings
– we no longer go out –
we bought new appliances
a grill, a blender
and my name on the doorbell since the day before yesterday.

Tolkien books and bills,
utility fees,
the flowers drink the sweat
that we exchange.

We go to our building's assembly
the lower floors are full of immigrants
they know that
we kiss each other
that you love me for my hair,
as their light wakes up your eyelids,

that our two male bodies
fit together
like war to the ancient world.

All this time that I was unemployed
I watered strawberry plants, orange trees on the balcony
I cleaned the windows every morning from
the dusty fingerprints.
On our pillows the evening
breaths
and we cook in the night
and your lips are so stained
that I will never regret offering you
my body.

Arachovis Street, Exarcheia

Between the avenue in the living room
and the little country road to the bathroom
shadows die in head-on collisions with my chest.

When I caressed the illuminated city of your hair
with your head a jancaea plant
in its steep rock
we displayed our verses like the broken tap to the plumber.
Your mouth a teaching room with open windows
the eyes two male lakes
with corpses of cars

we forgot tomorrow when your father arrives
with the bells that fall
in the heat of November
a smooth sound I dare say it is
like a shaved cheek.

Robin

It was no secret who Tim Drake was.
So many boys had the information.
I didn't usually trade toys or comic books,
I didn't usually have friends
or that young, gloved hand
deviously pressing my abdomen –
violently and beautifully panting me
the dark tufts of hair in his eyes,
the clear lines of his muscles
sketch by sketch terrorising my body.

I nudged my mum –
I like him,
I like this boy!
She kept drinking with the gang,
                    in Kefalari,
that night when I was ten years old
the first time I desired a body.

Stone marten

The living thing that frightened
the sleep of my first decade
walked with immense stature
on the rocks over my grandmother's house.
It was bleak with hairy arms
and a desire to see me dead.

Shady despite the light of the streets above
with its smile filled with ready teeth
it was just a village marten
and all this for one time when it came
and ate our hens
sneakily in winter.

So, a simple marten.

If you see it walking around
in your nightmares
shove it deep in the earth
deep-deep
before its nails pull you from your sheets
stark naked and rosy
like dead hens.

Frying oil

I dream of the invincible tree
                    in the red soil
but everything is dark
a statistical reduction of the population and an
elevator shaft with all its colour.

The touch cannot reach not even
the forecourt of randomness
and I am left measuring the performance
of my salaried afternoons
and the manager's raid
upsetting in the pan
the settled frying oil.

My head in your hand
a joystick of flesh
but I am waiting for thunder to bleed
and for the clockwork
storms and showers to come.

Holy bread

When the dictator's iron sword
falls in the central square
two tourists' heads split open
and a little sun lake shows
the good will existing
in the Employ of the Heavens.
And the nuns tall like socialist buildings
recall last year's Christmas;
time to bless the cherries and the berries
and the hands of gas salesmen who trade
flower bouquets for the deceived Polish women.
Now we bend our knee
the metaphysical bell erases baby cries
like bread that vanishes in the mouth.
I feel cursed
as if I played Jesus in a movie
and I am now ready to say
the big YES to Catholicism.

Warsaw, 8.7.2018 / 9.1.2019

Change of energy mix

> The first one who, having fenced a plot of land, thought to
> say: this is mine, and found people naïve enough to believe
> him, is the real founder of the Civil Society.
> Jean-Jacques Rousseau,
> *Discourse on the Origin and Basis of Inequality Among Men*

We focus on other things
the change of our goals
a simple
lignite phase-out in Western Macedonia

This sense that a future belongs to us
without seeing the stakes
they have struck into
our inner fields
this land divided
into properties
while our hands are drooping, wall calendars
on this bench of the coastal avenue
with the clouds that keep rushing forward
like dogs on a leash
becoming lamé streaks
over the boats on Thermaikos Bay.

Because we can't imagine
meetings without rivers
inside cut trees the game
of hide and seek
finding cover at the very moment
we are pushed the one inside the other.

And I see you're wearing brown
but your chest is not a tree
that one swells more slowly
you won't hear the panting
the sharp breaths.

Well, I put my arms around you
not the way you crush a grape in your hands
for some unclear, raging reason
and I give you
the plastic, square pot with the gerbera.
It's a fine cage for a flower.

Translated by Lena Kallegri

Marilena Papaioannou

Tale of a pandemic

Waiting/In the beginning

Yesterday we were the bare feet on a ship's deck, the wings of a bird, the lines of a notebook. We lived like a skirt hoop that can't find a sheltered place to unwind. We were the leaves of a basil plant, the scent of freshly baked bread, the prerequisites of a dream. We were what we were – anyway. Today we are drops of sweat that run down the forehead, a spring night spent before the TV screen; blisters on palms of the hands clutching the handles on the bus; marks on the faces of people who spend their nights awake at brave intensive care units. None of us has a single body anymore – we are just sums of swollen eyes, scratched knees and wounded hands. Today, yesterday and forever, we walk around upright, but deep inside we find myriads of reasons why we should slouch. And this is our strongest human trait – we love it for it is a part of us, albeit a painful one. Because it reminds us that our dream will forever be to live like birds, even though we know that they too live in clouds. However, there is nothing we demand; still we refuse to cry – it's dark and we cannot see beyond the end of our nose. We just keep waiting; living the eternal struggle. We are the eternal struggle. But this will never be enough – we know that; someday we may even get to admit it.

Unguarded cliff/Just after the beginning

The days will flow, the ferns will bend, the wheels will roll, the dances will come to an end. Summer will be lost, autumn will arrive, the eyelids will get heavy from the rain. Then winter will freeze everything – leaves on the trees, fingertips, nostrils, house walls, bodies, hearts. And nothing will be like you had imagined. People will have changed, words will have lost their meaning. Nobody will be dreaming of spring or waiting for the summer. Everyone will be afraid of the heat, pushing it away so that their insides won't flare up. They will have ceased to care, to touch, to kiss other lips. They will have forgotten the trembling of love, the white birds of eternal youth. They won't know where light can be found. They will feel totally lost. Without purpose in their lives, they won't know how to fill their lonely hours. They will keep saying: *The days flow, the ferns bend, the wheels roll, the dances come to an end.* And that is where they will stay. There will be nowhere else to go. Their heart will dry up, just like their land. Only the children may think of something. Maybe they will remember – they may have even been able not to forget. But they won't be able to change a lot of things – for they will be just kids. Just singing and dancing, screaming: *The days have flown, the ferns have bent, the wheels have rolled, the dances have come to an end.* And then they will start to fall off the cliff into the sea, one after another; and you won't be able to do anything about it.

Effort/Somewhere in the middle

Sometimes it's cold at night, sometimes it isn't. Sometimes you wear a double sweater, and sometimes just a T-shirt and summer shoes.

You gain and lose weight, just like you turn the bathroom light on and off; and with the same pace you flit over your phone. As if you were a serpent shedding its skin. Your temper changes every single time you blink. You haven't experienced such mood swings since you were a teen.

You constantly ask yourself – will it ever end? And then what? What kind of body will people have, what sort of eyes to look at the world with? Won't their hands be full of wounds? Will they be able to listen or will their ears have been sealed? What will they desire and what will they need? Will they be strong enough to dream? And what about the children's faces – how will they appear? Will they be scarred by the years added to their identity papers, without having really lived them?

Nobody knows.

One moment you need an answer, the next all you want is just to throw all the questions into a well of oblivion so that they will never bother you again.

You do hope, that's true. But you don't dream – and these two are vastly different.

You love, but never fall in love – no, that's a lie, this is the only thing you do. You fall in love, you keep falling in love – always and forever. This is your only trait, unalterable in time. Dead soldiers will be identified by their military tags – you, by the note you carry in the pocket of all your clothes, a note that reads 'died of lifelong love'. Well – it seems that you don't only hope after all, but you dream a bit as well. In this blur, however, in this ever-present doubt, you wonder if you had better not dream at all. As for the inactivity of hope – you can stand this. The effort of dreaming – no.

Time/Always in the middle

Time now constantly feels like the Day of the Dead. It is being counted in repeated units. It slips like water through your fingers, you cannot catch it. And more and more you realise that you really don't want to; you just want to let it glide over you as gently as possible, not letting it scare you – that's your only desire.

Or at least this is what you think.

Deep inside, you probably don't want to remember it. Scars – even if you end up with them – will be minor. Memory however – this is something you truly don't want. Remembering hurts; remembering annoys. Not everything in this life is meant for saving; most things should actually be forgotten. It's no use remembering joy when you can't experience it ever again. Or the scent of a peeled orange if you can't eat again. And of course there is absolutely no use remembering love – it's a complete disaster, if you can't feel the heat of another body around you.

And so you set a goal to change the scale of time. Such a grandiose plan – you know that. But you have a burning desire to change the counting standard. And if you can't eliminate the repeated units – seconds, minutes, hours, days, weeks, months, years – you will try to change their core quality. You won't be saying anymore *another minute passed*, but *another bird passed flying to its freedom*. You won't be saying *I'll meet you in an hour*, but *I'll meet you when the boat starts its return trip from the other side*.

You believe you can achieve that. But you also know you will believe it only till time stops mattering that much to you. For now, you keep counting, aiming to later undo this very counting, then to dream that you don't count and finally start again from scratch.

Till—

Small preparations/Towards the end

Just a few minutes remaining, the last miles that need to be covered; that's it, no more, the ship is almost here. Those who had left are coming back, those who had stayed are getting ready. Ovens are lit, tables are being set, bedrooms are tidied, clean sheets are placed on beds. Teeth are being brushed, hair combed and parted, lips coloured. Most hearts get warm.

The turbulent sea has now been defeated, the storm has almost ended – you can see it. But be cautious. Waves can appear in our country anytime, out of the blue.

You, the tallest of all, save a spot in the port for the short ones. Make some room for the weak, the small, those who oppose the return of the emigrants because of their fear. They too want to see all this, even though they don't admit it. They want to remember how the sea foam rises around the ship's prow; to hear again the sound of the ropes stretching. They want to remember the memory of a return they struggle not to forget.

But they're scared.

Don't reprimand them; be merciful. Tell them to do something simple at first. Let them wet their feet, let them put on their Sunday clothes. And then they can open the gates, set the animals free.

And don't forget to tell them to finally expel the dead; to push them into the sea; they shouldn't worry, some sailor will find them and lull them to sleep.

You just keep the kids around; kiss them, hug them – as if it is your first time, and for them the last.

Let's agree on the essentials/Is there an end?

Hustle in the street – finally. Children laughing, babies crying, dogs barking, blackbirds chirping, broken exhaust pipes, stray radio tunes, the neighbours in the opposite building making love, the ones next door killing each other.

Town squares are full of dreams again. Girls in their dresses, boys with cigarettes between their fingers, dust rising from under bike wheels everywhere. Fruit on the trees again, moisture on the roofs dried by the sun. Music all over the place. The sky colour changed, the day grew longer, new flower scents filled the air. The water became a little warmer, the skin more willing to touch. Hearts melted altogether, through the walls, some bravely reaching up to people's eyes, most of them however soon deflating – bravely as well. And dreams became dreams again.

Children became children again too – those were the ones who came to us and asked to make a deal.

That we will love again.

That we will give birth to sons and daughters; we will write songs; we will build houses and create gardens. That we will make thousands of plans. That we will learn everything again from scratch; that we will live even without measure, we will walk even without shoes.

But that we will never again do anything without love.

Translated by Christos Armando Gezos

Thomas Tsalapatis

The box

I have a small box in which someone is always being slaughtered.

A little larger than a shoebox. A little plainer than a cigar box. Don't know who, don't know whom, but they're slaughtering someone. You can't hear a sound (except when you do). I place it on the bookshelf, on the table when I want to spend time looking at it, away from the window so the sun won't discolour it; underneath my bed when I'm feeling naughty. They're slaughtering someone, even when we're having a party in our house, even on Sunday, even when it's raining.

When I found the box – I won't say how, won't say where – I brought it home, very satisfied. At first, I thought I'd be able to hear the sound of the sea. But no, in there, massacres are taking place.

I started to be sickened by the noise, the knowledge of the events, the acts inside the box. The box revolted me. I had to do something, to liberate myself, calm down, take a shower. I needed to take charge.

So, I mailed it to a friend. A friend I keep just for giving presents to. I wrapped the box in an innocently colourful cardboard, I tied the cardboard with an innocently colourful ribbon. Inside the mailbox there's a box and in that box they're slaughtering someone. Placed inside the mailbox, it's waiting to reach a friend. A friend I keep just to give presents to.

The first neighbourhood of Alba

In the first neighbourhood of Alba, the birds sink like stones into the sky. In the first neighbourhood of Alba, the one first to encounter and last to abandon. Here the uphill roads refuse to tilt downward. Here all routes are ten minutes long, all routes, regardless of the distance, the means of transportation, the rhythm of the gate, the speed of the vehicle. Always ten minutes long. Here, in the first neighbourhood of Alba.

Here trees grow naked. Grapes grow and age within hours. Juice, flesh, their lifespan condensed in seconds. Sometimes, during the days of quiet bloom, the clouds descend to touch the ground. They sink on seas, lakes, cups. It doesn't rain but pots and pans remain full.

***

The only certainty is that night also falls here
But only up to the middle
So,
The shorter you are
The longer you daybreak

***

In this instant, Alba sleeps its weary deep sleep
Here stone is prayer
And man
Is but a thread of miracles
Sewn on goodbye

This land

This land is given its funeral and buried deep down inside. A child is staring at the construction sites. Once he was a worker in these places, when he was older. Only a few things remain blurry. The memory of tomorrow's age, a scar on the hand, and perhaps, what this scar reminds him of.

Now the child with his two hands grabs his hand. The way birds in their sleep claw at the branches. Not to stop a fall, not to hold on, but just to grab all the flying left from their day.

City of loneliness

This neighbourhood is inhabited primarily by Nietzsches. Fatigued by their infinite return, lingering afar from good and evil, strolling romantic promenades, looking listlessly at idols and twilight, drawing moustaches on posters of Wagner, conversing aloud about the little hunchback, the eagle and the snake.

They kiss horses on the lips, they kiss time on the cheeks, they generally do what Nietzsches do. And dawn smiles with all its broken teeth.

One day, three Nietzsches were found murdered. Their bodies covered in knife wounds, their age untouched and all their apples eaten. Even when authorities allured to a revenge killing, we knew, with sufficient certainty, that this incident was far more important than a mere mention on the news.

[doors]

It was a night like all others. That night that we were robbed. All of us victims of the same plot, the same coordinated move. A shared occurrence. Our bewilderment an affirmation of their triumph, when the hand finds nothing to unlock, when the hand wanting to knock floats baffled in the void, when the menacing shoulder charges to push and you tumble.

It's because someone stole all the doors of this town. Simultaneously, suddenly and irretrievably. All of the doors of this town.

Wide-open buildings, privacy invaded, free passages. My belated sense of property.

In the morning we woke up numb. Space no longer held duration, there were no homeless and the children we kept secret played dazzled on the streets. A soft breeze caressed our nakedness.

We all then curtsied

To the ferocious dominance of chance

Words whispered to me by Franz Ferdinand of Austria

And possibly – he said – many of us
Will remain in History
Less likely as living
And rather as dead

I always said
It is the dead who are responsible
For the environmental pollution

It is horrific and there are thousands of them
Getting more
Minute by minute

They flood the roads, block the rivers,
Taking our places in the most beautiful restaurants.
Short-fused in the face of our slightest indifference
They stand there,
Silent and motionless, almost frozen,
Aggressively feigning disinterest.
Sitting – more often aground –
Sneering at our choices with their perpetual assertion.
Creatures celebratory in our grief,
Sorrowful in our joy
The ones we proclaimed our opposites.

Musical,
Frail,
And mostly,

Philatelists.

The day I invaded Denmark

Possibly by lack of measure, enthusiasm surplus
(or simply boredom)
I decided to invade Denmark

I armed my decision

With muskets and horns
Drums, bayonet
And a rhythmical trot.
I folded my sleep
To fit in my pockets
And for my coat of arms I choose
A slaughtered age

***

Before break of dawn
I am on my way
Covering the distance
Covering the distance
To Denmark

***

And there they are:
Guardians of ruins behind enemy punches,
Owners of rare seashells underneath umbrellas.
Girls plucking seconds, women kneading months.

Look, men dying in foreign languages
And I walk in silence.
For so many years I walk in silence
Covering my distance
To Denmark.

***

One morning I crossed the final frontier.
Armed to the teeth, I invaded Denmark.
The streets with Danish flags
The homes with Danish kids
The time with Danish hours.

I invaded and invaded
This country
They all call Denmark.

***

***

And found her empty.

***

***

People abandoned the cities, the villages and the streets.
Perhaps they caught wind of my plans
Or perhaps they got fed up being Danes
– Empty cities, villages and streets –
Surrounded by silence.

***

And the water,

Even the water

flowing soundlessly

***

One night, on a sudden square I met a figure:

'You are Hans Christian Andersen,' I said. 'You are a Dane.'
'So they say' said he. 'They talk too much. And then they go silent.
But don't fear the silence. There once was a time when silence was
another way to admit that you know. And now we experience this,
her domesticated behaviour.
'We lived time, helping our dreams seek shelter in some stranger's
sleep, in fear we might suddenly wake up. Perhaps one day. When
the white page ceases to be silent. When the space between the
words thickens or when the sky loses its height.

***

But enough of that. Take this axe, take it and hold it tight by the
     handle.
Take it and let's go take down
ancient trees.'

Translated by Elena Mastromauro

SERBIA

Danilo Lučić

Discipline of a symbol charger

Your love for me is crawfish and seashells
my memories are blades

to someone, we'll seem like a labyrinth:
inside of you, me that I hate,
although you are the one who from within me hates the inside of
    you

it's that time of the year when the air sparkles
if someone said dark
that's because it was dark

repetitions kill
how can something that used to be a tree have legs

semi-automatic hugs
a man winters on another body

truce has come and gone
I was forgotten in the trenches

Big fire. Hungry fire.
Fire for all of us.

Exhausted and still, she reached out for me •
I accepted the embrace so that in my neck she can feel
the blood boiling • and how in my sweat there is no medical stench • so
with her dying breath she laughed and said 'It's alright, honey, it's alright'.

• my happiness is when I feed the dying woman • change her clothes • cause
only then I am alive • only then I am human • I know
that one day they will move me out never to return
• I remember *where were you when in death someone gave birth to a mother*

because we write about her • and she doesn't complicate she only
multiplies • the wort par tare not the cries tearing the night • but
those unbearable silences that explode after them • when you don't know
what to do and how anymore • hands are broken • eyes are hollow

deep in the night • invisible suite comes through the door
• lining up along the walls • as if praising the tortured woman
with their smiles • lady of the ceremony is the last to arrive • elegantly
she will cut the line • and cries will announce the celebration

Ibid,
53.

Where from and, more importantly, why do these people pop up from that fog of absence years or decades after they disappeared from our lives I know that they, with their changed personalities and faces or maybe only seemingly different because of the moment when they once again make themselves known carry a message and meaning directed only to us that they themselves are obviously blissfully unaware of so they bring it to us unknowingly Lately one such man carries a letter for me almost every day but I still don't know how to read it I fear he may be a warning for my transgressions and it pains me that he walks so self-righteously through my days He doesn't even see me on the pavement in the shop on the bus in front of the building by the park on the stairs If one of these days I approach him with a benevolent smile and kill him will the envelope open and the message reach the fearful recipient.

ULYSSES' CAT

There comes a day, spilled and dry • everything grows stiff like darkness
beasts don't stalk me, nor do I • I've got nothing to say
under the heaven • I only feel good when I eat
and scratch • funny how only in silence all things come to you

actually, the best thing in the world is hearing you're alive • concurrent
to the laughter of a child or clicking of the Zippo lighter cap •
this way I can be carefree and dead • with an olive oil
smile • you draw a perfect circle in the sand with a twig • a wave wipes it clean

again you draw a perfect circle in the sand with a twig • why not •
and why should I have to articulate when I can just
watch a woman knitting • freedom is not to be able and allowed
but to not be obliged • I am just an extra of emptiness

satisfied with my pay • what if up there the depths are
actually empty • who is going to have the last laugh •
like a madman • the sun is setting, and I am smiling
• this day has turned into a giant stomach

Shelves for text objects

and it was a horrible winter in her cold
room naked floors and poor man's light
bulbs

on my heart a fingernail grows

I promise, in the greatest darkness
without a torch I will find my way to
you

you squeal like the death of a mouse
where do you live now? there? and how's life? I can't
anymore don't close the jaws just yet
as soon as I find the acts on insides
don't touch me like scratchy velvet

astrology of poetry is relentless:
soon it will approach the absolute text
and after that the absolute art

before you lies a cheetah in an open cage

Katarina Mitrović

For you, a flower that is white

She had to go on a trip
for a
psychiatry conference
and she said:
'I'll be back in two weeks.'
I waited
rode my bicycle talked
to the dead went to the
cemetery that was
empty
quiet
peaceful
sad
on a little stone wall
embracing the spilled earth
I'm not lighting a cigarette for my dad
finally accepting
there's no mouth he could smoke with
hoping
somewhere up there he isn't calling me names
because everyone else is getting their cigarettes
and smoking except for him.
Unbearable emptiness
nests in my throat

I'm visualising my organs
the moving heart
the brain placed behind my eyes carved
and slimy
one kidney
two kidneys
blood streaming through the body
I'm feeling all that
but the emptiness is still there
I'm looking at the wet earth
saying:
'Fuck you.'
And I remember that last day
when his eyes became like those of
a child of
a doe
tender
in our flat
a man in a white coat
was standing next to him
I don't know what he was saying
it looked like he was just opening his mouth
the nurse was wearing clogs
I was terrified at the sound of her tapping
around the living room
they could all go fuck themselves
that bald doctor
blinking behind the glasses
that fat nurse
with her loud clogs
sinking into my clean carpet

her thin socks
her fat legs
why are they coming and saying all
those horrible words
I hated that they were saying all that
in front of him
he isn't a child and he understands everything I
wanted to
protect him and say:
Fuck off.
Disgusting doctors with their diagnoses
that I hate
and those big white diapers that
made father look awkward he
upset me and was guilty of
getting cancer and giving up
I went to the kitchen took lexilium
my body shook
because of my revolting desire
to get it over with already.
Brother played The Drina March turned
up the volume
shouted around the house to encourage him even
though we knew
dad would tell him to piss off if he could
which made mum say:
'Turn that goddamn music off.'
We were like three lost children
in a crowded street
brother called a priest
although my father wasn't a religious man

when he was given sacramental bread
there came a few moments of fear that
he wouldn't open his mouth despite
everything
I needed to believe
how he would go to heaven he
must have thought that too
he opened his mouth painfully and slowly the
piece of bread melted on his tongue
I watched him get smaller at
least it looked like that and
the priest said:
'There is a prayer that helps the
soul leave the body.'
We were trying to decide
if he would read it
in other words
if father would live
we weren't sure what you were supposed to say in
such moments
brother was looking at mother
who was looking at me
who was looking at father
who was looking at the open window
fresh air flew in
it started to rain
at that exact moment
I was choking on the realisation
that my father was dying
and I couldn't help him.
Someone put down an icon of the Virgin Mary

while the priest
was reading a prayer
I didn't know how to set my father free
from this situation
if I drove them all away
maybe he would get up and he'd be alright he
and I live the way we want
he and I know how to enjoy
mother was stroking his head
the way grown-ups stroke sick
children
brother allowed himself to cry
all over father's face
I desperately needed to piss
but that was one of those moments
when you know
you'll miss something important if you leave.
He was looking around the room all the
fear had vanished
when the prayer was over my dad
for days almost paralyzed sat up
in his bed
looked up and died
it looked like a miracle I
believed in God then and
asked him
asked him really nicely
to send dad to a good place hoping I
would end up there too.
The ambulance
didn't arrive for two hours

which was enough time to
think of a combination to dress
him in:
yellow shirt
brown velvet pants leather
vest
and red sneakers
those were his favourite clothes my
tears were weirdly big
in his wardrobe there was
a hidden
envelope with money in it
dad was still lying in the same place in the
living room
having the need to hug him I
approached the body
that was once my father and
realised how that was just an
immobile shell
not meant for hugging.
People from the funeral home arrived and
sent me
to watch over the oak coffin in
front of the building
although I didn't know who'd steal it brother
ordered that particular one because it
reminded him of
what father was like

Translated by Kruna Petrić

Maša Seničić

Tiny rampant beasts

Evenings get colder and, here in the suburbs,
my room is overlooking the landscapes
from which embassies rise in pain. I endorse it.
The children of diplomats inhabit surrounding parks:
their tone intimidating, almost violent,
and their hands, well, obedient.

Rows of recently imported cars lie secured
behind the gates; such a comforting sight.
The officer smokes, a respectable convention,
while a domestic cat is running wild, finally free,
chased by furious, no one's hounds.

The government is recruiting thousands of so-called
'border hunters' to patrol its razor-wire boundary fence;
Recruits must be 18 and pass a psychological test.

The cat squeals in a slow, poetic manner.
The weather is pleasant. The dogs' jaws are bloody,
its paws dirty, heavy, mindless.
My neighbours, they sleep tight,
their jaws tired of well-prepared,
well-deserved food.
The lovely beast had escaped, they notice.

Underneath the conformists' homes, the badlands reign;
does it frighten them, or does it keep them alive?

During a recruiting fair at a police proving ground here,
a gaggle of teenagers ogled a display of machine guns,
batons and riot gear.

Suspicion perishes, in the form of a cat, tenderness
locked inside its belly – death itself must be bored
to death. Mother makes a healthy breakfast.
The kids in the park, they are clueless, religiously
walking to all future lives, classrooms and marriages.
'My stomach hurts again,' I tell my caring parent.
She laughs. But cold little bodies, truly, make me sick.

The new border hunters will augment their efforts, officials say,
by pairing with more experienced officers to spot migrants
from towers and vehicles, track them and ultimately
put them back behind the fence.

My family is charming, my professors patient:
they chase me around open spaces to show me
the path. I breathe loudly and scratch the edges.
My lungs widen and become a desert.
I am not courageous, just partially quiet,
which is why they depart satisfied,
with jaws full of sand.

A glossy flier held out the promise of rugged patrols in 4x4s,
super-cool equipment to detect body heat,
night-vision goggle and migrant-sniffing dogs.

'I am my parents' and my lovers' tiny beasts,
divided into inconsistent, disquiet particles.
My hands are beasts,
feeding my unborn children,
also beasts, brought up on parking lots
and imprisoned among the same, adored by the same
and devoured by the same' – I say to the
a small domesticated carnivorous mammal.

A 17-year-old at the border hunters recruitment drive
in this midsize city, is eager to graduate high school next year,
he said, and then become a border hunter to 'defend his country'.

A glossy flier held out the promise of an undisturbed life:
super-precise equipment to detect cats running scared.
The dead little creature stares at me.
It starts to smell.

Budapest

humid continental with warm or very warm summers

the city is trembling
for people are sleeping in its railway stations
and crawling underneath the metro lines,
secretly building houses and palaces
where they would talk and eat and survive
without ever being seen

night-time temperatures are very pleasant,
especially in the residential suburbs

European borders are guarding
the empire of human frights,
its poetics of passing through
is teaching kids to be rude and proud
while maintaining the confectioneries
as hideouts for the conformists
they will surely become

Mediterranean depressions moving above the inversion

there are exactly twelve people
with red turtleneck sweaters,
it must be a decent concert hall
in which I hid myself from rain;
twelve, I count recklessly, I count again
I, countlessly, get wet anyway

sudden heavy showers also occur,

they could be anyone, these red spots
exhaling while applauding underneath my feet,
then continuing to their cars on parking lots
and ugly fountains inside lovely inner yards

westerly winds bring mild oceanic air

international students are getting drunk and bored,
their exchange programmes kindly approved

by the institutions avowedly claiming freedom;
what is future, but an institution doing the same

thunderstorms, some of them violent
with heavy gusts and torrential rainfall,

in front of the pools an old man is reading,
he could be the calmest one in the universe,
with no need for towels or any other service

the fog can last for weeks

the furious festival youth
is rushing towards discount treats,
the old man raises his head
when he sees me standing in line
to step into a hole filled with water
nights get colder and the first frost arrives

he must know about the palaces underneath
the twelve red turtleneck sweaters,
the bookstores that change places
and barbershops looking like theatres!
he raises his head, guarding this void
and never entering it, this old man,
he must be the city itself

winters are variable and unpredictable

A heavy black cloud

the rest of the world is yet to be discovered
by aircrafts and lovely two-headed
children of islanders:
this strange piece of ground breathes salty,
offering me other people's backyards
and a shelter from the definite

hungry dogs keep barking
until the sunrise leans onto cable cars
so the sky could rest its itchy feet
and its murky edges;
I remain detached

the legend about the dead kingdom
reaches up to the mainland:
did you know the Royals were ants
climbing onto the sugar-apples,
eating and inhabiting their insides?
sugarcane on top of the cupboard
is slowly being devoured by their Highness,
hundreds of little black slaves
getting their sweet revenge
by claiming the territory of
Moradia Pena

the coordinates are
a question of stomach
whilst the legs must
obey to divine gravity;

/

both are keeping me calm
and both are keeping me
here

concrete stone blocks are
trembling under incoming waves:
constructed as part of defence
they arise from the docks like
an unprepared army

the ocean is tenderly treating
catering facilities on its shores:
it splashes them with kindness
and lavish food leftovers while
empty swimming pools echo
this land's history:
greedy tourists forget
their body parts on the cliffs
and continue to cruisers,
relieved, permanently hungry;
their impatient youngsters,
made by mistake,
await at family homes,
made with great caution

below rocky coastline
seascapes gently place
their bloody feet: mornings
first touch the mountaintops,
then roll down to the water
in which they drown
to become dusk

pulling my hair
across these unknown depths
will make it easier for you to love me;
having sand underneath my tongue
will make it easier for me to gracefully
wreck on my innerscapes

on tips of my fingers I'll grow
these fruits I've never seen before,
foreign herbs and weeds will crawl up
my legs up to my mouth
where they'll eat each other
and leave me to choke on the remains;
on tips of my fingers I'll grow
a different kind of lowlands,
towards which we'll walk discreetly,
to the point of eating each other
and leaving this island
to choke on our bones

solid boulderstones reign
under the museum-like spaces
cluttered with pebblestones:
warm and sharp, unremitting rocks
remind me of millions of stitches
requested for a unique piece of cloth

I could be a stone or a piece of land
designed as foundation for
a navy-blue hotel with tiny balconies
attached to its tired body;

I could be one of the cliffs
to put in the pocket just in case
you need to fall, quickly and quietly,
or in case you need something
to dip in your milk and then accidentally
break teeth on its edges

I'm a house overlooking the piers,
my backbone dilapidated
and my sides unimaginatively
sand-coloured;
above my head, a huge sign lingers
though my dead colonial parents
didn't bother to teach me the language:
'vende-se' must mean I am
one of a kind, an untouched jewel
of this poor and windy shore;
I'm a house on sale,
brought up to be a beauty
and left to moulder unmarried:
a womb prudently depicted
and provided with upmarket furniture
never to be used again

I dreamt of my father,
carrying his mother up the streets of Funchal:
her feet are sore, her skirt is obsolete,
her memories are a mountain;
the car mechanic smiles at me:
my tyres are flat, my knees are bruised,
my memories are whimsical;

the one thing that comforts me is that
from wherever I stand I can feel the ocean:
its face swollen, its peace intimidating

I've come all this way
solely to point fingers at another place
I won't ever consider a home:
I forgot when everything was
and where and why and where

That land, it doesn't exist

I

Tue, July 2, 08:47h
Is water in Cyprus safe to drink?
People also ask:
Is English widely spoken in Cyprus?
Is Cyprus a poor country?
Is Cyprus a third world country?
Is Cyprus a good country?
What religion is Cyprus?
Is Cyprus its own country?
Why is Cyprus still divided?

II

'That land, it doesn't exist' –
Someone said, referring to a land we are standing on.

There is of course a better way to talk about the land:
About its plant life, its colonial architecture, its owners.

I touch a home, abandoned: the stone underneath my palms
Is acting like sandpaper: it leaves a bloody trace when touched,
And if forgotten: it becomes a monument.

International youth group fighting for climate change
Is gathering under the scorching sun: subtropical climate
Makes you obedient. That's why four German poets
Enter a cathedral but exit from a mosque,
Barefoot.

II

'A poet must know' –
Someone said, referring to neglected places.
But a poet doesn't have to know anything other than
What he sees: a giant bird gently being carried
In the arms of a foreigner.

There are European goals to be achieved, they tell us.
What I hear is: *clean water clean water clean water* and
It makes me think about soldiers cutting hair on the borders in
    the heat.
They must be thirsty. I imagine being a hotel expanding all the
    180 km
Across the land, accepting no one at my gates.

Ceasefire is a lovely word, but in the end – how can
Being together be a natural state of affairs?

I ask not as a person but as a landscape, as a back street:
They are always so quiet.

Srđan Srdić

About a door

I could write a word or two about that little one, and how he stands before a door. It was Saturday, going on for six, the little one had arrived and stood there, nothing else was happening. I don't know who could find this significant and what might be written about nothing. The little one was nondescript, but such was the time as well, history found itself in a rift, sizzling with all kinds of follies. Many stand before many a door, there is nothing new or special to it, people and doors have been written about: it is not an exceptional topic. I am rather well informed about that kid. Twenty years have elapsed since then, I am not certain, however, that time matters much. Time both passes and does not pass, both exists and does not exist. The same is true of that little one, there, he exists anew, exactly as he used to be, whether it is twenty years or less is all the same. Whether it is he himself makes no difference, since I see what I see. People believe what they want to believe, not that they are desirous of other things beyond measure. They can trust me too, nothing will change if they do, I will recount what I wish. Let them do whatever they want with it. There is paper and there is fire and that is all there is. The little one slept in a big room. The thing with the door happened in spring, which is fair to mention, so as not to look down on the kid with unnecessary pity, because it wasn't cold in the room that morning, but it was gloomy, the boy could still make out: a bed, another bed and yet another one, a table, a wardrobe, a mirror. Noteworthy objects, and their silhouettes. The longer you are in the dark, the better you are at discerning things, which is no trifling advantage. The little one found it hard to get up before five, which he never came to terms with, it would be right to remark that there is something evil and sadistic in the voices you hear at that time, the voices that have to tell you this and that. I wouldn't say that the number of those who would listen at that time is too large, nor is the number of those who would listen at all too large, but there are stories and that is it, nothing can ever change the fact of the story, because there is no interest to it, none whatsoever. No one expects anything from a story, no one wise. Some voices were heard from the dark, which was a usual occurrence, otherwise the little one wouldn't get up, someone had to do that for him, the people from that house are dead today, and probably it is the same with the house, and it is painful to remember all those dead people from the dead house after so many years, perhaps twenty, perhaps less. The rest is a lie, long-term memory distorts, and what remains is not even semblance, it is other than what it used to be, a story that is not important, for if it were important, people wouldn't die, neither would houses die. Since everything is equally significant and insignificant, even the kid before the door is equally a story, whatever opinion one would have of it. It is possible to tell billions of stories about that little one, there were things there, but he himself would opt for a few, if he had to make any choice, because beyond the chosen stories lies calculated sense, and there is hope of the existence of calculated sense, and the hope arouses thought about stories as messages to be deciphered before it's too late, as if anyone would benefit from them. The trouble with the story about the door lies in the fact that nothing happened, and the sooner we all acknowledge this, the sooner we will give up storytelling illusions. The little one stood there, the world also stood, and this lasted a while, an image of this has remained, which is a story, and all this is about that image/story. The story about the door is an apology of any conceivable stasis, if it has to be anything at all. Even today at that very place is the door, the river, the small bridge, the electro-technical school, the high school, the court, the Youth Club, the museum, the access roads, the red kiosks, the bike racks, the whole lot is still there. River, concrete and lawns. Children from the school buildings run along the river, until it turns too cold to run. Some of them run, others look at them calling out remarks, all this around the river is rather intensive. On this particular morning I would write about, no one was there. It was different in winter, prisoners were brought out to clean the snow from the bridge, monitored by guards armed with automatic guns. They reached the town market later on (if I am not mistaken, the market is no longer where it used to be, but I couldn't swear to it) and kept on cleaning, as the village vendors who came to work first insulted them, shouting: 'Boo convicts, boo bandits, it serves you right, fiends!' Hard-working folk they are, with a proverbial high opinion of themselves, those vendors working in such a manner. Again, no one thinks the best of the river, although it has no smell that wouldn't be in direct relation to people and their affairs, the crowd, however, passes by and swears at the river with a common aside to the effect that only a couple of other places have a similar odour: the dog pound and the starch factory. So, the little one heard one of those voices, once alive, and he followed it. Old age suffused the adjacent room, he passed through it sullenly, in the bathroom he washed and partially roused, he washed his hands with a bar of yellow children's soap (only this soap was used in that house, until it disappeared [which is good for the principle of association]) and he squeezed the Kolynos toothpaste onto his brush (only this toothpaste was used in that house, until it disappeared [which is also very good]). He rinsed his mouth, returned to the kitchen, sat down and leant on the table, tea with indistinctly sweetish taste was already there, and next to the full mug scrambled eggs were steaming, looking appetizing, but the little one didn't feel like breakfast, he had about ten minutes to do so many things, rushing about exhausted and perturbed in the sense of feasibility and ultimate effect. That's why he did this: he sprinkled half the contents of the saltshaker onto the plate with the scrambled eggs, rose and went back to the dark room where he got dressed in no time, it sometimes so happened that he slept the night in the clothes he'd worn the previous day, but this was not such a night, as the morning was not as any other, at least he always thought there was something extraordinary in that, there, before the door. Behind the door was supposed to be music, and this is what he hoped for when he first arrived in this town, it was supposed to be the town of music, unlike the town in which he was born and raised, where there was no music, there was no such music, there was not enough music, this is why he cherished hopes that he would find music in a new town, but it isn't always easy with hopes. He had arrived and for months now he'd been struggling to convince himself that he was not mistaken, that music was everywhere, that that was the right music, but this wasn't the case, music was elsewhere, in different places and with different people, behind the door some people squirmed, he got to know them, shortly afterward his interest in most of them waned, and a similar fate befell the fake town of music, or the town of fake music. Some sort of music was heard there and music experts ascended the stairs clutching printed notes in their hands, obedient students following in their wake, thinking they would acquire the privileges of music, which was not happening, and there were also those apathetic when it came to music, most often they didn't feel like anything, so they morosely observed the world out of the music cage. Of all disappointments, and their sum total is certainly not small, which a random objective calculation will show, the greatest is disappointment in music, when it occurs, and when it actually occurs, one stays in a noisy, deafened space, which is a paradox, but a true paradox, and against this paradox one can do nothing whatsoever. The little one stood before a mirror, it was unlike later before the door, on the other side of the door there could easily be nothing, whereas with the mirror it was completely different, this is why he liked to stand before the mirror, in winter, in the afternoon, it was dark outside, and in the depth of the mirror it wasn't dark, which delighted and encouraged him. He looked at the clock, it was a solid Soviet clock, a present from a man now dead, the time was approaching, he took the box with his instrument and started on his way. The voices greeted him cordially, their owners were alive at the time, and there seemed to be no surprises to brace oneself for. However, the knowledge of the fake music in the fake town of music was indeed a surprise to get prepared for, but who would know this, so now it was necessary to suffer in the school of music, and such boys never suffer, they resist and think they have all possible rights and that they are isolated from the craved outcomes which they await in secret, in no time at all they turn into revolt per se, raving and confronting the illogical construction they qualify as the system, and they do so in order to pay knightly deference to the object of their own animosity. The little one shut the gate behind him and went on to catch the train, trains have an advantage over people, they are indifferent toward the urges of leaving, coming and arriving, there were not many trains back then, only a few would steal out of the historical rift, and the little one had to wake up before five so as to successfully catch one of the rare trains and get there in time for the Saturday orchestra rehearsal, because, for all the lies about music, he was dedicated to the duty the music suggested, and he didn't want to betray it, as it was gradually betraying him, turning its back on him mercilessly. To be better than music, it was a strong argument when it came to the showdown of self-reconsideration. He comprehended this a month before the event at the door, he kept trying to play a modern French composition, a vibrant solo de concours, he wasn't even close to success, but he sensed he knew what it was supposed to be like, and that on the other side there were those who sounded successful but felt nothing, he was brimming with this intuitive achievement, shut inside a sterile classroom for individual instrumental instruction, upstairs, on the second floor, the left wing of the corridor, he lifted a window shutter and spotted kayakers pushing hard away down the river in their elongated vessels, elegant, powerful and handsome. It was worthwhile sticking it out until the end of March, everything was to change then, and it was possible to avoid the waiting room, up until then it was cold, those who waited smoked, wrapping in newspaper sheets something that wasn't regular tobacco, playing cards, worn Hungarian cards showering across laid pigskin bags. As soon as the first April days came, passengers waited for trains sprawling on the station platform, the boy occupied a place on the corroded railing remains, and out of habit I kept turning my head in the direction of the north, where the railway signal was changed, announcing the arrival of a train. A man's day was born out of hubbub, the boy reasoned, squeezed between workers, villagers, and passengers, overhearing the tongues rattling against the palates and filling-studded cavities, it seemed to him that he was invisible, and the invisibility was good, like the mild sun on the neighbouring fields. The rhythm of the train like morphine and like blue-green and like steam from sometime machines used for paving periphery crossroads. The boy tried not to lose his footing as a reflex action, he didn't need to, he couldn't fall, because he didn't have anywhere to fall, people cancelled the laws of physics, you couldn't leave and get to a place where there wasn't a human language, because you thought in a human language which was hopeless, but without which you couldn't even be hopeless, you couldn't be anything, I knew that, even then I knew. And there was a piano: a badly tuned piano, a classroom on the ground floor, and there the little one made it his habit to pursue his search for forcefully interrupted dreams, the piano was man's friend, for it sounded without too much invested effort, touch was all that was needed, tone was touch, there was no question there about the quality of tone as aesthetically decisive, the quality of touch, the touch drawn in the eardrum. The kid would do this when he was early, he would enter the classroom, remove the lid from the piano and touch it, nothing else, because you could do nothing else if you wanted your dreams back, the plan would have to look exactly like this. And the train was slow and it was slowing down, the suburbs, tilting hangars, industrial landscapes for accustomed observers, nine kilometres in linguistic secretions, nine kilometres to the fake town of fake music, times nine in return and nine the next day and the day after, perhaps not on Sundays and perhaps not on some other days. I longed for air. The door was opened, the train was in motion, despite the metal warning signs, no one paid heed, Moses was anachronism, those in the front jumped out chased by the mania of urgency, deftly, skilfully, landing on their feet and going on toward hospitals, markets and smoky, distant contours. The little one extricated himself so as not to be seen, even though no one noticed him, who cared, and the little one crept in between the freight wagons, jumping over their couplings by means of safety handles, it smelt of coal and serious poverty. When he crossed over (he duly paused and glanced left and right, although there were no trains at all) I started over the embankment, there were other ways as well, even better ones, but he chose this one, and he stuck to it, since even then the little one's character was unwavering, conservative in decisions he held for a certain reason to be correct, an unfaltering, fanatically and stubbornly consistent type. The absence of people and sounds started right after passing the embankment, I cannot say I noticed it immediately, it could easily be a projection caused by the time distance and the wish to write the effects that were actually missing, but that determine the story structurally (and semantically, inevitably). Still, in the maze of streets down which he had to plunge in order to reach the school, the little one passed the university, a butcher's, he liked to loiter in front of butcher shops and count the pieces of bacon on hooks and piled sausages, he passed by a pub where students of mechanical engineering studied, and by a dark house entwined in ivy, in that house and its damp, depressive yard he would find a student of Italian and her elder sister, he would spend an afternoon with them, they would laugh, he would leave and not forget any of that, this would happen three years after the day I am writing about, I recall it clearly, but I can by no means gather why I recall it, of all the things I could have memorized, why this and what it all means, when you remember it and recount it on. Then, there were the prison walls, it was once known that the prison was where the court was, there was no transport for those with escape on their minds, fustiness, lichen, and countless stories about what went on behind the walls, the little one had an inkling of it, of the solitary confinement cell, of the attic and the basement, the Sunday soup made from prison pigeons, two Hungarian watchmen and an insane colossus of a guard, who insisted on working night shifts, so as to welcome ruffians, rapists and irate alcoholics eagerly, and beat them bloodthirstily without witnesses, investigators and record-keepers. When one stands opposite the court façade, the school seems to be in a luminous depression, surrounded on all sides by buildings taller and more monumental, shadowy and stately: the school looks as if it had sunk into something, slipped into all those melodies buried in its history. Viewed from the bridge this depression is even more pronounced, and the little one wondered whether the real secret, what it was that was painfully difficult to fathom, was in the depths of the river, rather than behind the door of such an insignificant and worthless building. From that very bridge, which is merely a strictly functional steel monster, descend some steps, the little one went that way, and I heard my own steps, it was Saturday, and it was early, and it was the first time I'd heard anything in that noisy, deafened space, on the paved path leading up to the semicircular concourse in front of the door. I walked on leisurely, and a flash of the only just risen sun leant on my shoulders, crisscrossing the cold school façade, as if only then did the little one become wide awake, he raised his head and stopped, at first almost bumping into the door decorated with tall, iron figures. I know no one who has heard the sun, or colours, or smells, or shadows, but I can confirm that all this could be heard then, there, there was nothing else, the little one kept spinning in wonder, searching for the place where all this was coming from, but there was nothing, and in the nothing was heard the sun, and melodic colours, and shadows. The boy took another half-step and touched the door, which usually opened easily, I'd done that so many times, but nothing happened this time, one couldn't go any further, and I stayed there, before the door, alone, many people consider possibilities, this is one of the possibilities, solitude, absolute solitude, it is also a possibility, but as a theory, as a draft or a logical resultant, because there appears perplexity, one wonders: how am I to know who I am if there is no one else, and there was no one else there, someone had locked the door and forgot about it, someone who didn't expect that anyone like me existed. What else could anyone be but a totality of relations, whereas there, before the door, there was no such intimacy, I stood in a membrane that had suppressed the world, swelling with light, not heat, not winter light, but only light, only from the effect which shaped scenes and spaces and without which there was not even that trifling nothing with which I was left before the door. The second time I almost thrust at the door, disconsolate, not because I looked forward to what was behind, but because absolute solitude was equal to absolute deafness, I muttered a chain of meaningful syllables and they didn't find adequate sense, because they were addressed to no one, and they couldn't be addressed to me, because I was nothing, like all that piled stone around, lawns and indifferent trees, syllables and words ceased on the inside of the membrane, bursting, fragmentizing, vanishing. So I stood before the door, I could go back, toward the safe place where I'd come from, to search for trains and their tracks, wherever they led, wagons and embankments, to recall, that above all else, but I didn't recall anything, and then there was nothing, when you could recall nothing and no one, there was no movement and no way back, toward the trains and tracks. The boy standing still, the door standing still, the world standing still, and they in it, the world-membrane which everyone had forgotten and which had forgotten to inhabit itself with concepts, notions and beings, I found myself there, with my instrument, my useless instrument, a whistle that did not announce itself in tone, since tone was duration, vibration in time, and time had cancelled itself, annulled itself, for me to stay there all by myself before that door, all on my own, man was seldom less than that. And I cannot say that it lasted, because it didn't last, and it did last, if it hadn't lasted, I couldn't recall it, and I couldn't invent it and write it down, the boy stood, not anticipating anything about the man writing about the boy who didn't know anything about him, but he knew that there was a door through which you couldn't pass, and you were made to stand and wait for another man to write another door, the one through which people and boys passed, covering the same different ways, you waited for a man with the right words, with passwords and codes for people, boys, women, girls, alive as well as the dead, what was, what wasn't, what could have been and what would never, never, never be. The sun behind the back, the river. Paper, fire, and everything there is.

Translated by Nataša Srdić

Goran Stamenić

we sat in front of the big house
where snakes sleep under the doorstep
I was a great liar in the
blackberry bush

secretly like an anthill and quietly
the dark sun sits on my lap
all is confused and I am everything
all the things are wondering people:
the nose of the airplane full of withered grass
falls on your nape
and spreads its scent in the flames
all of a sudden, life turns to longing
outside of reach
of your tiny golden hand
sky for the wounded hawk
stumbling through the undergrowth

that's what I meant
when I said

*

you walk carefully, as if you invented
the high-noon shadow
I have a spell for you

if you are touched by a golden star
a particularly attractive light
you hear
the willows sway dreamily
and what the other mary saw in the garden

from our plantations towers rise
in that moment, anything could be a threat:
a swarm of holly bees lives
on your skin
shimmering matter of light crossed
with the shadow in the treetop
and the branches tired
of full-blooded cherries
at night, anja plucks every other eyebrow
we returned to the forest
with no one telling us to
there's something built there, like a tongue,
which means clumsy –
a tongue dreaming of a mouth

the city reproduces through the outbursts of flu
you know how snakes spread their jaws
you know how there are snakes we haven't even named yet
you know how hard it is to swallow a whole apple
still green to the touch

*

hiding in fake orchards
like a man inside a man –
you take off your clothes full of crickets

you're afraid that the great truths
can only lead you forward:
at dusk we have forgotten
to put oil on your nape
hell will be filled with you

dark sun sits on your lap
a hand inside you spreads its branches like
the lower nile, you feel
in your nudity how mysterious are
the putrid orchards
between the bone and the flesh
in towers among apples
you don't need a king to be
queen

*

following a trail of friends who
departed while it was still dark, you approach
the lake
that for some reason glows
the clouds turned their colour into sugar
and are now melting in the sun

following a trail of friends, your foot
is already under the water
like home, it's cold
you step into the grove's mirror
filling your pockets with rust

just like the cape of the afternoon relieves
your august fever
nothing is hiding behind the lake's intent
to swallow you –
it's clear
like a ball of light
somewhere in your body
where there's the most blood

*

you already know that everything happens at noon
tuesday, machines devour wheat
anja imagines symmetrical things
human dream of progress slowly crumbles away
on the mirror of its own fatigue

wednesday nights are spent at the olympus of work
carefully gathering morsels of silence
someone turns the pillow over to the cooler side:
silence is a body in the mines of kongo

a machine plucks every other willow from its root
the only thing that's certain is that someone
is trying to convince us of something
leaving us blinking like a newly hatched
pigeon

I

only through tears you'll see the sun
tattered bloody banners of clouds
sprinkling water on the skin of garden workers
and nothing else

darkness shall be so barren, ancient
unknown to the terrifying words
your joy, doubted for a moment
will write a poor man's anthem:
the world trembles like the arms carrying a hero

the world is a wound on the body of christ
at the coast where nothing rises
blunt waves shall cover your feet
and your face shall be wet

II

as soon as you looked away
god built a basement for you
and left you in the darkness with oranges
all flammable

in the morning, the only thing
you'd smell from under there would be roses
and you'd follow the sound of bullets down the macadam

in your dream you lit
a flame to see yourself

in that same fire
you forged the nails.

III

we can't tell for sure why the waves are glorious
while we plunge our naked bodies
over the rocks

and we sing cause the horizon is always
so flat, and we sing of the sun
when it steps over it

in sunset there is no doubt that everything is everything
that weak hands hold the weak world
and tremble

we are sure that the waves tear down, build,
tear down
the flat continent
on such honesty

on being hidden

now I am south, now I am further south
border guards tell me mountains grow every day
around the muddy valley, like a tooth still rotting upwards from
    the flesh
over them the fishermen throw wide nets of smoke from the airplanes

weaving the ladder that with the first step
falls to powdered sugar: you fall
tipsy and sleepy co-pilots live for the minute of flight over mirdita
like a father over the crib of his newborn child, looking for a
    glance returned
met by sharp, foreign world. nothing can be seen there
co-pilots fall, and that's more than a youth's dream, pulling
    mountains to himself
like a riverbed seen from the bridge, how did the fruit fall before
    gravity –
the only way to descend among the joyous.

first year of magic

at least I'm a glorious peasant woman plucking coriander from her
    garden
and all the coriander asleep in the heavens of her mouth, bathed
    with o lives
I am born this year when things are born, dogwood, blackberry,
wild things that leave my face a mess, things that are all but things,
things that are figs
in such a garden thousand tiny angels can be planted
and their cross-eyed sisters
that by autumn turn golden, full of bees, they learn that štator is
    september
squeeze out the honey-spell from the bud, the noble lindens, the
    stream
crawling uphill to its spring, the cauldron of black light
where bees finally pour honey into the first year of magic

A1

highway crumbles when, a blink ahead of us,
bride's stone appears. by the end of the road hikers are resting in a
    church
prayers have long been written on the rocks in these parts
so that rivers would flow through the bushes
bringing forth beds of green bulbs,
so that someone would cut down the dynasty of rocks and
    gymnosperms
more sleepy than an army of crickets caught in resin
prayers for the magic of solemn children, their sweaters and the
    soles of their feet
so that it may all last and end and start again:
our tiresome roaming through other people's valleys
eyes return to the bottom just in time to see
north narrowing down and suddenly vanishing from view.

Translated by Vesna Stamenković

Vitomirka Trebovac

opposites

in front of the
'olga petrov'
retirement home
a man kissed
a woman's hand
she raised her head
and he blushed
and what happened after
I don't know
because the wheels of my bicycle
are big
and I'm
already in another part of town.
here it begins to rain lightly and
there is the stink of mcdonalds
a girl plays accordion in front of it
stiff families eye her suspiciously.
I would crush
them with my big bicycle,
but I am polite as well
my upbringing does not let me
cause any issues.

I will never forget

some woman reading proust
on a tram in gdansk
and a fat cat who
ate my pancakes when
I was a child
I will not forget
how mum screamed
when they told her something over the phone
and the view
of the skyscrapers from some hotel
I will never forget
the waiting line for visas
and how we played frisbee
drunk in a park in berlin
before dawn
then I will never forget
how they helped uncle to escape the army
because the war began
and my grandma's hands shaking
I will never forget when sara was born
and I was at the pool
first second third
emigration
I will not forget
when I saw you
on the staircase of the bookstore.
never.

scar

maybe I've already said
that I had three friends
one liked Russians
one Americans
and the third was so-so
he didn't know whether to go
left or right
and he's still like that
anyway
once when we
were children
I beat them in a street race
to the lamp post
(and they were in a good shape)
I touched the post and collapsed.
now I have a scar, a small one,
in the middle of my forehead
I wear it like a trophy through life.

walking

s. and I wandered away a couple of times
yesterday at the cemetery
and we barely made it to the funeral.
we took a strange route
three kilometres on foot
through terrible mud

and we mostly talked about
gaudy gravestones
odd last names
about the fight from the previous day
he said that
the grass is really nice here
and I agreed
but the whole time
we were walking
I was thinking
how the saddest thing in death
is not the death itself
but a sunny day
compared to a dark grave.

about old age

maybe one should not write
about old age
and about me bathing you
and how you were ashamed
because I touched
your decayed body and freckled skin
with your downcast eyes
powerless
you suddenly
talked about how your feet
were small and charming
and how now

one should die
but not even that is easy
while you were talking
the smell of a sharpened pencil
overtook me
and I see my childhood self at once
I'm sitting at my desk,
sharpening my pencil,
but the lead keeps falling out
then I remember
that my feet today
are small and charming
I got that from you
I thought
I shut the water off
and hug your
bony
weak body
my grandmother little girl
maybe this is not
a poem about old age.

Translated by Tamara Božić

SLOVENIA

Dejan Koban

alga mechanism

the children will be the last to know
it won't hurt them
it will be a beautiful day when the last one dies
he will choke on a toy in his throat
from this day forward no one will know
what the word play means

I.

hands will fall
the marbles won't find their way
there won't be anyone at the road sign
because all mankind will chant
in the stadium that they want to revive the butterfly
and travel the seconds to a small eternity

the pins at the end of the polygon will fall down
they were without numbers
no one was able to calculate their losses

the ace was too far and too pawned

the parade pointed to the rifts between the performers
flags were flying less enthusiastically than last year

147

we assume that we revolve around the basilica
swallowing up the devoted wedding guests
and endless honeycombs

no one will be able to help the children
to stand up straight and step forward

the birds gaped through their beaks
left speechless by the force of the single thrust

we break in through bricked-up windows
we will sprinkle more opportunities on the ground
maybe someone or something falls for our trick
we watch safely through the morning fog

the game will play out till the end

everything is ready for the imminent blossoming

the monster falls between the ribs of our tiny offspring

there is nothing more we can do

we can't move anything anymore

we can only turn around and leave

the end is here

the world continues beyond

II.

the silence extends through our swollen pores
increasingly quietly
and it is thoroughly glazed into memory

silence covers the sand that fathers pour down our throats
so as not to reveal the annulled prophecies

we decided to dissolve the fire ourselves
and leave through abandoned cities

there are hidden stories all around
awaiting our curious wrinkles

we may simply be tiny lost ones
soon we will moor at the dock of a dreamy land

no one survives in the sky of cut-out eyes

the air covers the mucus of foreign body

schizophrenia is our only ally

who steals poultry at night
but only leaves us rotten eggs

we are writing a long list

all the names and surnames are known

all names and surnames
are our names
and our surnames

no one is protesting

octopus

the sky descends through the sound of a drilling machine
corals are stored in the core
pedestrians smile
and tremble in the same second
war may undulate again
words are too heavy
swings of arms too often
simplified into a foundation
the door can no longer close all the way
we are doomed to the wind
troops of disabled people ride the ramps
we are strong in making momentary decisions
a cyclone is inevitably born in a glass of water

flawless execution

conviction drags itself into abandoned quarters
of screams where it can slowly start
fulfilling its task

to make a wall overgrown with purple lichen out of
a man conviction never doubts itself
and is good at selling itself to characters
who lost the Russian roulette vacuum
shivers and wants to penetrate from the plasma
of hovering vacuum wants and makes war
side by side with conviction together they could
perhaps one day manage to seal the edge
of the closing line and jump over the crazy locomotives
which neigh at stations and tear each other's
bellies and ruffled obscenity conviction
and vacuum measure the drain canal of their
country and they guffaw and guffaw
their lungs inaudibly shamelessly letting out
the last atoms of oxygen

settled bill

our bodies are slowly becoming
transparent through them hands
slip away tremblingly learning grammar and
forgiveness spring arched its
back people let their grey
faces into the sea fright is present
but the wind forces into reckless
actions hands follow it becoming
dragons without reins and the thin red line
hasn't for a long time now marked the first
front line

inner body machine

when two pairs of human eyes stare
long enough to see through the texture of bodies
all fear still innocent and primal
can end time and begins the last
countdown to absolute zero
probably a lot of important things
happens in an imperfect line between
possibility and desire one thing is certain
turtles cannot love through their shells
but they can save a world that is desperately gasping
for shelter symbioses appearing one after another
from case to case forest breathes
loneliness castles howl from inner
cold train compositions tremble
above the surface of the earth two pairs of eyes
still calmly exploring the texture
of eyelid decorations under a loosened man

we breathe more slowly but much more decisively

Translated by Petra Meterc

Kristina Kočan

bronze over the plain

like a dark curtain rises
the sky's wheel of blackish
their glinting speckles
it shadows all underneath from nothing
dips in the wind wildly
the cyclone swathes thought
in feathery lace a phantom
body with a song stolen or
used or borrowed
which can fall silent in a trice
hums with rapacious roaring
toward the grapes the last raspberries
when bronze flows over
the plain the maize still resists
the weight of its cobs pointed belfries
ring out near and far away
poplars sway under
an iridescent fluttering membrane
in the ear they are accompanied by tunes
of scythes from the Old Continent into the New World
as part of a millionaire's plan
to introduce all birds
from Shakespeare to America in 1890
eighty pairs of starlings

to Central Park what can they
have seen where did they shelter
what tree did they perch on
the tree-hollow dwellers how did they form a wave
for their murmuration what sun
did they see was it for them
that the bronze light spilled

to comb the coast

every day to guide
sluggish feet
straight to the wide
coast beyond distance
is not in steps merely
in thoughts suddenly
to conquer to listen
to northern birds winds
to furrow the face
to comb the coast
with ageing hands
to dig in the sand
to seek and find the new-old
an inflatable doll a wooden
clog a wheel buoys
fishing boxes helmets
shoes Persil boots
an earring cigarette packs
torn nets lobster

traps ropes
for infinity to seek
find not so much
to have various
bottles inside
hundreds of messages
including
call me with a
phone number
most of them written
in a child's hand
with utmost hope
where an address is given in white
nights to write back with
tremulous fingers
your letter
arrived in a faraway
land all the way here
never to have
only to seek
to meet people
without their being there
not only on islands
everything washes up everywhere
only when and where
not after high tide but earlier
to march in a trance
homeward with the day's finds
into the night and into a new
morning seeking

brushwood

crunching snow under shoes
falling behind is
the warm hut the fire
is slowly dying
satiety of sighs
rubbing of moist bodies
on a still afternoon
in the murk smouldering soft-stepping
deer in the brushwood
entwined tracks fingers
flames which spark off
words on warm tongues
only winter sprouts
instantly swallowed
by kisses
on the way ahead

asters

in the sultry
waning day
asters
persist
flycatchers
orange-tailed
swarming above
in the air snatching
small warm bugs
all is blending
in green and brown
only asters
in their rigid dance
of bright colours
are shining through
not to be forgotten
by birds
over winter

Translated by Nada Marija Grošelj

Davorin Lenko

A secret chord

'You know what I was always afraid of?'

'What?'

'When you were going out, out drinking ... I was afraid that you'd come back one night, or morning, walk naked into our room, wake me up and say: "Sleep with me now or we're finished."'

'What made you scared of that? I mean, you know I ...'

'You were out partying. Drinking. God knows what else ... I was scared the time would come when you'd return, at just the right level of restless and aroused that—'

'And you wouldn't be able to? Or want to?'

'Not sure. Both, probably. And you'd end it. All thanks to some banal cocktail of hormones and chemicals ... Can I ask you something?'

'What?'

'Did we ever actually come close to that?'

'Yeah ... we did, as a matter of fact.'

'What stopped you?'

'You were sleeping. Waiting for me. With the light left on ... you weren't to know what was going on inside me, were you? You weren't to know what I thought I might get, but didn't.'

'I sensed it.'

'Did it hurt you?'

'Of course it did.'

'I'm sorry ...'

'It's ... You don't have anything to apologise for. You didn't ...'

'If you were ever to find out ...'

'I'm not interested. Really, I'm not.'

'That's fine. It still doesn't mean that I'm not hurting inside though. That it doesn't eat away at me. Now, when I see ...'

'But I really am happy that you started drinking at home.'

'Are you?'

'Yeah. You don't need company, an audience ... You're ... You're just you, as you are.'

'But is that really me?'

'I don't know. It seems like it. Feels like it.'

'Why didn't you ever get me drunk at home? Force me to stay in?'

'Force ... I don't want to force you into anything. But I did try to show you ... And you know yourself that it didn't work. You went looking for others. Whilst I was still focusing on anniversaries, you were always bringing someone else along. And then we'd each drink way too much, each in our own way. Then we'd try something, give up and ... the whole thing would start all over again.'

'You should have got me drunk at home.'

'Yeah ... I know. But also – I don't know. I don't know why I didn't keep trying.'

'It probably wouldn't have worked. I had to go out, get away. To new things, to new people ...'

'You didn't give me the chance to love you. And I wanted to love you ... but you didn't let me. You weren't there. You should have been, but instead of you there was, well – nothing. Emptiness. I was genuinely afraid that you were going to give me an ultimatum.'

'What would you have done?'

'Nothing. Well, other than pack my things.'

'Just like that, so final?'

'This is serious stuff.'

'Yeah ... but anyway ... My glass is empty. Look ...'

'Top it up.'

'What with?'

'Whatever you like.'

'No. You tell me.'

'Just ... Whatever you fancy.'

'Do you prefer kissing me after whiskey or wine?'

'Whiskey.'

'I'll have whiskey then. Whiskey's great ... well, wine is too.'

'I don't think wine does you any good.'

'In what sense?'

'You get really sentimental.'

'Do I?'

'Yes.'

'What about brandy?'

'It suits you. You glow.'

'Did I exist before alcohol, do you reckon?'

'Of course you did.'

'What was I like?'

'In many ways ... just like you are now. Drink doesn't change you as much as you think ...'

'What was I like as a kid?'

'What were you like? I don't know.'

'Neither do I anymore. I'd like to see some pictures.'

'Now?'

'No. Not now. One day. Never mind. It's not as if ...'

'Ash, is something bothering you?'

'You. You're bothering me.'

'Because of the lump?'

'Yeah. What else?'

'We'll find out more tomorrow.'

'Mhm.'

'And then we'll go from there.'

'Have you any idea of just how brave you are?'

'Do I have a choice?'

'It'd drive me crazy ... Waiting like that.'

'But anyway ...'

'Do you even find me attractive anymore?'

'Of course I do. Why do you ask?'

'It's nice to hear it.'

'When I come home and catch the scent of your shoes in the hall ... The smell of your feet in those shoes, I mean ... I don't know ... But that's how I know that I'm home.'

'I've put weight on.'

'Four kilos you said, yeah. And that's nothing. How much do you weigh?'

'Erm ... Too much.'

'In any case, I don't care at all.'

'Really?'

'Really. Well, look ... if you gained another sixty I might. I'll be honest. But now ...'

'I fucking love you ...'

'You too. You too, Ash ...'

'I mean, look ... Eventually we'll have to face up to it ... I've got drink issues, you're ill. Most likely, right ... All I'm saying is: we'll have to face up to it eventually.'

'But so what if you drink?'

'Why don't you judge me? It seems like you ought to ...'

'No ... I won't. Why would I? You're at home. With me. Within reach. You keep on enjoying yourself. I've waited long enough for this ... I won't let you go. Not just like that.'

'Jesus, you're every drunken woman's dream ...'

'You're not a bad person, you're not violent ... you like a chat. If you ask me, we're better now than we were ten years ago.'

'As much as I love him, I'm glad he's left home ...'

'Yeah. I agree.'

'I don't have to pretend anymore.'

'No.'

'What I'm wondering is why I deserve all this ... Shouldn't I be ...?'

'What?'

'Punished?'

'But what for?'

'For everything ...'

'But Ash, that's ... You never caused anyone any harm. Do you know that? No one.'

'I put you through all of my ... All those nights when I wasn't there.'

'But that was then. It's over now.'

'Yeah, now I drink at home.'

'And there's nothing wrong with that.'

'Do you really still love me?'

'I love you. And if this counts for anything: I love you more than I did ten years ago. Like I already told you ...'

'What about ten years before that? And another ten?'

'We were completely different people back then. What did we know? Who even were we? Not us.'

'You're right. Not us. God ... Back then I had some sort of phallic obsession with bottled beer.'

'I remember ... You could be so funny with that.'

'How childish we were ... in every possible sense.'

'And do you know what? I'm glad that ... Well, I feel better now than I did when we were first together.'

'How do you mean, better?'

'More ... myself. I'm a bit clearer on what I want, who I am ...'

'Your fifties: the new twenties.'

'Or thirties ...'

'Yeah. For me ... I'm not sure. Were things actually better then? Worse? I don't know.'

'Do you remember how much make-up you used to put on? And how you dressed?'

'As if I wanted to ... I don't know what.'

'Me neither. But that's the way it was. And then that last time when we went round to Lara's ... do you remember that?'

'Yeah. What about it?'

'Nothing. You went barefoot, and in that ripped T-shirt ... That's the kind of freedom teenagers bang on about. But what they don't know is that they've got just a little longer to wait. A couple of decades. There's so much pressure on young people ... Just look at what it did to us.'

'But did you like me back then as well? At Lara's?'

'Yeah. You were feisty. Really feisty. You were glowing.'

'I was drunk.'

'That was the day I discovered the lump.'

'Jesus ... That was the day?'

'Yep. Life and death ...'

'I don't want you to be the death.'

'Neither do I ... but right now I don't have a choice. We don't have enough details to draw any sort of conclusions yet though.'

'Tomorrow.'

'Tomorrow.'

'Will you be alright to drive yourself to the hospital?'

'Of course I will ...'

'Because I won't be able to cope without ... But can I go with you?'

'Please, yes.'

'Have you told the lad?'

'No. No point in worrying him over nothing.'

'Yeah ... And listen: you do know that getting absolutely out of it is not something I enjoy? Do you know that?'

'I do. I know.'

'But that means that sometimes I drink when I don't even feel like it. And that other times I don't drink as much as I would like to.'

'I know ... And whilst we're on the subject, I'm going to tell you something. Something rather ... it's a tough one.'

'Tell me. Just say it.'

'I enjoy buying alcohol for you. Well, not "enjoy", but ... it arouses me.'

'Why?'

'Because it's so ... Well, dirty. But also because I love you.'

'Jees ... *that* is hot!'

'...'

'...'

'I enjoy taking care of you. In a way that I can and know how.'

'I'm tainted. Whichever way you look at it – I am.'

'Not everywhere. Not at home. Ash, maybe that smell of alcohol, and your drinking, and everything that comes and exists between us ... Maybe that's the real soul of a family, the one people preach about.'

'Only they don't get too bogged down in the details.'

'Because ... yeah. Do you know what someone said to me recently? That religions are just a basis for individual spiritual growth. To help you better find your place in the world. You have to find your own way, though – and your basis can be good or bad. Same goes for what sustains you along the way.'

'What's that got to do with ...?'

'With you? Us? Maybe because something which is generally considered *forbidden*, taboo, is not necessarily a bad thing. Not if you've followed your own path to arrive at that point. But if you launch yourself into it without walking the path, then ... It's like learning to swim. Slowly does it. And on the other hand, there's the type of person who's never seen the sea or a pool in their life and jumps right into the water anyway.'

'Do you think I ought to seek treatment?'

'No. I really don't see the need for it at the moment. I do think, though, that you ought not to trouble yourself with that stuff as much.'

'Fuck ... I never imagined ... I never imagined I'd have a family. Let alone one like this.'

'But that's just it – we're perfectly fine. Aren't we?'

'In a way, yes, we actually are.'

'Before you started drinking at home ... It was as if you wanted to prove something. I don't know what, and even less so to whom ... Do you even know yourself?'

'No. Maybe I did back then.'

'But it's not like that anymore ... You don't try to prove yourself anymore.'

'Don't I?'

'And that, to me, is incredibly hot. You are yourself. You're becoming more and more yourself. And your eyes ... your eyes have a sparkle; they're alive. Most people who drink have that empty, distant look about them, but you don't. And yeah, now and again you look absent, I admit – but absence ... despite the absence, your eyes keep their sparkle. As if you were in a really beautiful place. And I'd love to know where that is and where you are and how you're doing there and ... And I wonder ... And I look at you ... At your drinking ... That's what it's like: I don't see it as the enemy. As something that's come between us and tearing us apart ... No. You are who you are. It's how you are. It's what you became, and the more I look at you, the more it seems that you feel okay. In yourself, I mean. In the person that you've become. In the body that you ...'

'I was looking at myself in the mirror recently. I really don't look bad at all for an alcoholic.'

'I don't like that word, you know.'

'For a woman who drinks, then.'

'And do you know what else? What if they don't find anything? If they find something benign? Or just a small swelling of some kind?'

'What then?'

'I don't know ... I'm scared that we'll lose what we have now ...'

'We won't lose it ... We can't. We're in too deep.'

'You think so?'

'I know so. Tell me something else ... Why do you like me?'

'There really is something wrong with you today ...'

'Yes. There is. Because of tomorrow.'

'I don't know what to say to you ... I like you because you're not one of those women who has a couple of glasses of wine and gets all crazy and needy and thinks that every fucking thing in this world revolves around them.'

'Yep ...'

'Because those women scare me.'

'I know. Are you scared of me?'

'Not anymore. Not anymore.'

'Do you ever think about my pussy? About all the places she's been? What they've done to her?'

'I think about it. Yeah.'

'Would you like me to tell you?'

'No. I think I know enough. I don't need that.'

'Fine. But, shit, you know what ... I have to tell you anyway. Do you know when that rock-bottom moment was? Not for me, though. For you. Only, you don't know it yet. You can't, because I haven't told you. Hm ... Rock-bottom was when you had that car accident. Remember?'

'Obviously.'

'You know how you couldn't get through to me? I saw you were ringing me, but I couldn't pick up ... I couldn't. Didn't want to ... I was having sex. He was pulling me by the hair, while you kept on ringing and ringing. It started to get annoying and I took the phone off the bedside table and saw that it was you. And ... and some huge wave of panic came over me. Disappointment, even. Because you'd shattered the moment I was having. Why were you bothering me? Right now, at this moment when I was really letting myself go? When I was totally out of control? And why you, of all people? I can still see myself now. But don't think, by the way, that I remember him. The guy. If that helps at all. I can see myself there, on the bed, on all fours, face in the mattress because I didn't know what to do. "Is it important?" he asked and I said something like: "No, just my husband", and he took the phone and threw it across the room, it went flying and stopped making a noise and he thrust himself back inside me and I ... I was ... happy ... in my own way, yeah. Because he made the decision for me.'

'Could be worse, I guess.'

'Could it?'

'You could have answered the phone.'

'Some women do that, I know. Out of sheer rebellion or spite or something ... I don't know. But I wouldn't do that. Ever. It sounds strange but ... I always loved you. Throughout it all. I'd never have done such a thing to you.'

'I know that, now. I know. Thank you.'

'There's a bottom to every bottle. You know what my lowest moment was? It seems like a good time to tell you, for my sake too. It was when someone turned me down for being too old.'

'You were good-looking when you were younger. Now you're beautiful.'

'Go on, stroke my ego some more.'

'Really? Ok, you know what I like?'

'What?'

'Your teeth.'

'Oh god ... these?'

'They're hot. And I want you to know. They're not perfect. And they're hot.'

'What else?'

'Your cigarettes. Want to know the real reason why I stopped smoking? To improve my sense of smell of taste. So that I could better ... Well, smell and taste you. One other thing. I like it when I kiss you ... and you taste like tobacco. That's hot too.'

'Jees ... Anything else?'

'Remember last time, when I got all worked up in the middle of the day?'

'Yeah. What was it?'

'You ripped your top.'

'That was it?'

'Let me finish. It's a little thing that says something about everything else. About your teeth, too. You ripped your top on some branches or rose bushes, I don't know, it doesn't even matter. And yeah, it turned me on. Why do you think people sell ripped jeans? But those are already ripped, designed to be ripped. You ripped that white top yourself. In the garden. When you were working. There's a big difference.'

'Is that how you love me? Ripped?'

'Yes. From life. Ash – why did you stick with me?'

'Because ... Jesus, I don't even know ... please don't be offended. It was more that I felt ... More that I ... You know what I'm trying to say. I started to feel closer to you. Those episodes ... It was like they gave me an energy. For myself and for us. It's not easy, and even I still don't exactly know how and why ... But I'm sure of it. And I get you. More and more as time goes on, but I'm scared that I wouldn't, if I wasn't off my head all the time. Ironic, right? I read this book recently, the title escapes me ... And there was this scene which I thought was really beautiful. Some woman had a partner and a lover, and the two of them bump into each other on various occasions, but her partner always managed to run away – avoided the situation. And one time the lover asks him why he so obviously avoids him, and he replies: "Because I can see a man that I'll never be. Not to her." I mean ... if that's not love, then I don't know what is.'

'Yeah, that's beautiful ...'

'He wanted to be everything, all of those roles, to arouse a whole spectrum in her ...'

'But you can't be a partner and a lover at the same time.'

'No. And he knows that he can't. He just can't. That it's actually just not possible. And yet the burden of it all eats him alive.'

'To me, it's not about possession. Or trust, either. Or *betrayal*. It's basically about sex.'

'In what way?'

'As the thing that hurts the most.'

'With lovers, you mean? People who I slept with once and never saw again?'

'Yeah. With those people.'

'If it counts for anything ... I never wanted you to suffer. I really didn't want that.'

'Yeah, well that pain is not unpleasant.'

'You found it pleasant?'

'Well, "pleasant" ... deep. Deep and dark ... When I think about you with other people, I physically feel sick. Physically – in my stomach. But I know that ... Well, I know that at least, if nothing else, that I care. That what I feel for you is real and deep. Pain doesn't lie. I slowly started to accept it. And with it, you as well. Look ...'

'Go on.'

'I'll never get over how I could never give you an orgasm.'

'But you did ...'

'Yeah but not with ...'

'No. Not that way, no. But so what?'

'Ash ... it's like this ... for a long time love was something I grew to know, and now it is known. I love you.'

'And I love you too. And I think ... I think I'd like to make love to you tonight. Really make love, not just have sex.'

'What about the lump? And all that it entails?'

'But that's just it. I'd like to feel you, as you are. As you are now. I'd like to feel your death. To feel your death and suck the life out of it.'

Translated by Olivia Hellewell

Tomo Podstenšek

Bobby

We should have been going on holiday, we even had the plane tickets and a room in a hotel already paid for; Monika had bought a new bathing suit and I sunglasses, suntan lotion and a few other bits and bobs. Then a few days before our departure, my mother told me that my father had had a small stroke. And although the doctors were saying he would make a full recovery, it seemed to me that I should visit them.

On the day of departure, I first drove Monika to the airport. We both knew that, by a network of coincidences, the blood clot which had blocked the artery in my father's brain had also sealed the fate of our marriage. The holiday together was supposed to have been a last desperate attempt to see whether we could save it or not. For close on two years we had been living almost separate lives, we had separate bedrooms and – although we didn't talk about this – we were seeing other people now and then. At least, I knew that I was and, from various clues, I guessed that Monika was too.

Most of the time in the car, we didn't speak. Neither of us felt awkward because of this, we were used to it. I wasn't annoyed with her for going to Malaga without me. It even seemed sensible: it was too late to cancel the trip and it would be a shame to let a paid-for holiday go to waste.

Even when I told her that I had to visit my parents because of my father, I didn't think or expect that she'd go with me. In truth, she had never been particularly close to my family. In truth, they didn't even like each other, not even a little – now I could finally admit it. And we would be splitting up very soon, which meant that they would probably never see each other again. Nobody would be sad because of that. Nobody apart from me would even give it a second thought.

After forty minutes driving Monika asked me if I could stop at a service area. I turned off at the first opportunity and waited in the car. During stops, I always wait in the car. I didn't ask her if she wanted to go to the toilet, or to smoke a cigarette, or whether she just wanted to stretch her legs. It didn't matter, it was all the same to me. After a few minutes, she returned with a bottle of water and a bag of crisps, and we drove on.

When I dropped her at the terminal and helped her take her suitcase from the boot, we both knew.

'So, that's that,' she said.

'Yes. Take care of yourself.'

'You, too. I hope your dad will be alright.'

I nodded and turned away. I had several hours driving ahead of me and wanted to arrive before dark. I didn't think much about my ex-wife to be; our goodbye had been easier than I expected. Like scratching off a scab that has long ago dried up and comes off without the slightest discomfort. The skin underneath remains slightly pink for some time, and then that also disappears. I wasn't angry with her, I had no reason to be – I was just as much at fault for the failure of our marriage as she was. Probably more so. Now it was no longer of any importance.

I did envy her slightly, being able to walk alone along sandy Spanish beaches. Perhaps to get involved with some drunken English tourist with a tattoo of a bulldog on his biceps. A shame that the stroke had not affected her mother or father instead, I thought childishly. Then I would be the one now waiting to board the plane, and by the evening I'd already be sipping a cocktail in one of the numerous bars and flirting with some pretty Eastern European tourist, young enough to be my daughter.

Instead of that, for two weeks I would be squeezed into my childhood bedroom, which had long ago become a junk room, full of cardboard boxes containing things that no one would even look at again, but which my parents, for some reason, thought it would be a shame to throw away. At the very thought of breakfasts, lunches and dinners together I lost my appetite. I just hoped that my father was alright enough so that I wouldn't have to help him dress, wash and so on. I wasn't very close to my family, either. In truth, we didn't like each other all that much, we kept in touch out of habit, and out of a sense of propriety and obligation.

The motorway was almost empty, the temperature in the car set at a pleasant twenty-one degrees. I turned the radio up and put my foot down. The music was interrupted now and again by traffic information. Somewhere at the other end of the country, someone had once again driven the wrong way on the motorway, and in Srednja Gorca there was a warning of a dog wandering on the road. I reached out and picked up the half-empty plastic bottle that Monika had left on the passenger seat. When I squeezed it, the thin plastic crackled slightly. Holding the steering wheel with one hand, I awkwardly unscrewed the cap and took a few sips.

***

I remembered how we used to drive to the seaside every year – eight or nine hours trundling along the old road in a car without air conditioning. Of course, at that time I didn't know that something like air conditioning for cars even existed. A good job, too, or I'd have gone mad. We would set off at four in the morning to avoid the worst of the heat and to make maximum use of the first day of holiday. In the end, we almost always got stuck in long lines of cars carrying holidaymakers who'd had the same idea.

We always stayed in the same place on the Adriatic coast, where the company that employed my father owned a group of holiday homes for employees to use. We weren't in the same chalet every year, but it wouldn't have mattered if we were, for they were all almost identical.

From the small hallway, there was a door to the left to the bathroom and straight on was a larger space with a kitchen on one side and on the other a sofa bed on which my parents slept. I slept in the small room opposite the bathroom, where there was space only for a narrow bunk bed. We would put our suitcases and luggage on the lower bunk, and I slept on the upper one. In the main room there was also a door that opened onto a small terrace, with a plastic table and a few chairs.

It was a good ten minutes' walk to the sea through a caravan park and pine woods. The beach was mainly stony and without any facilities. Some parts had been covered with uneven layers of concrete. The sea was always murky and on the surface floated bunches of sea grass that stuck to your shoulders unpleasantly when you were swimming. Every ten metres or so there were large concrete pipes from which poured waste water from the hotels we could see on the other side of the bay.

When we were on holiday there was a much stricter and more precise timetable than when we were at home. My father had a very clear idea how holidays should be spent and what needed to be ticked off for a person to rest and relax. Out of bed at seven, to the shop for bread, then a quick breakfast on the terrace; after breakfast down to the beach and an obligatory half hour lying on the towels that we spread out on the patches of concrete and weighted down with stones so that they wouldn't blow away. Then the first swim, followed by anointment with suntan lotion, sunbathing, then the second swim, and once again anointment and sunbathing. Around noon, back to the chalet, cooking lunch, after lunch coffee on the terrace and a rest, then at about half past three back to the beach and once again alternating swimming and sunbathing until the evening. In between, an ice cream. Once a week, we took the tourist train to the nearest town, where we walked the stone-paved streets, looked at the remains of the town walls, visited the aquarium and bought postcards and souvenirs for our relatives.

Every year exactly the same. Except for that summer when we had Bobby.

Bobby was a stray, the mongrel offspring of a mongrel mum and mongrel dad, a small, shaggy and undistinguished dog, with a long, unkempt, dirty brown coat. His hairy tail hung to one side, his left ear stood upright, but his right ear hung down. He had a slightly too short lower jaw, so that his upper teeth showed and it looked as if he was laughing the whole time.

On the second morning of our holiday he wandered onto the terrace of our chalet, and because my father threw him a piece of sausage, he stayed.

At first, I was a little afraid of him, as I wasn't used to dogs; my mother was convinced that animals did not belong in apartments and my father shared her opinion. But the dog was young and playful and after an hour or so, we had become friends.

The next two weeks, Bobby accompanied our every step. He went with us to the beach, although he was very scared of the waves and didn't like to go in the sea. When we were in the chalet, he would lie around on the terrace and patiently wait for someone to show willing and play with him. If you threw a stick or a pine cone for him, he was happy to keep fetching it back ad infinitum, and that summer my shoulder really hurt.

We fed him on leftovers and put water for him in a rectangular plastic ice cream container. I improvised a lead from a length of blue, plastic-covered washing line, on which I led him around, although it wasn't really necessary, as he followed me faithfully the whole time and never went far from my legs.

It turned out that he was also very intelligent and that he could quickly remember – if a suitable prize was on offer, of course – various commands. After a few days, he already responded to 'sit', 'lie', 'wait', 'find' and 'fuck off', which were the words my father used to drive him off whenever he began to lick his salty feet when he was sunbathing on the beach.

It's interesting that I couldn't remember who had given him the name Bobby. Nor could I remember the dog doing anything really naughty. Just little things. When it was high tide, he would yelp at the waves. Once he went after a seagull, but of course he didn't catch it. And another time he chewed my mum's flip flops, but he didn't completely destroy them. That year, I was always first up and checked whether there was any dog mess on the terrace that needed to be flicked underneath the pine trees and hidden from my parents. I was hoping that we could keep Bobby if he behaved well enough.

And when we were getting ready to go home, it really seemed that we would: my mother spread out a towel on the back seat next to me and my father kept telling me that I had to make sure the mutt stayed still while we were driving.

At first, Bobby kept turning his head in fright and looking around him, but then he calmed down. As we drove, I stroked the brush-like hairs behind his ears, which he particularly liked. But he didn't like being stroked under his chin – perhaps he had some kind of complex about his short lower jaw.

After a while, it became ever hotter in the car, Bobby began to pant faster and his tongue was hanging from his mouth the whole time. On the sly, I kept pouring a little water from a plastic bottle into my palm and when he licked it, he looked noticeably better. His breathing also became more regular.

'I need a wee,' I lied nevertheless, so that we stopped as soon as possible.

After a few kilometres, my father really did pull off the road and we got out of the car. My mother began to unwrap the sandwiches she had made for the journey and my father pressed the tyres with his foot, to see if they were properly pumped up, while Bobby sniffed in the bushes.

We ate our sandwiches and then it was time to drive on. When I called Bobby, my father gripped my shoulder, pushed me into the car and said tersely: 'Bobby's not coming with us.'

Then he slammed the door before Bobby could jump into the car.

'Clear off!' he shouted at him and shoved him with his foot. Because the dog was still whining and running around the car, my father bent over and picked up some stones. When he threw the first one, he missed by a mile and Bobby, who thought they were playing, went chasing down the slope after the stone to bring it back.

'Stupid mutt,' my father quickly got behind the steering wheel, put the car in gear and pressed the accelerator.

I turned round, but because of all the suitcases, bags and folding sunbeds that were crammed into the back of the car, I couldn't see through the rear window how Bobby was left standing in a cloud of dust with a stone in his mouth, unable to understand what had just happened.

***

When I saw my father, I was still somewhat shaken. He looked several years older, his left eyelid and the corner of his mouth were drooping slightly, so that he looked like a wax dummy that had been placed too close to the fire and had begun to melt slightly.

'The doctor says that after a few months of rehabilitation he'll be as good as new,' my mother guessed what I was thinking.

My father just mumbled something and lit another cigarette. I noticed that his left hand was also failing to obey him completely. I was trying not to stare too obviously or show my discomfort.

'There was no need for you to come,' he said unclearly, and if I didn't know that he'd recently had a stroke, I'd have been sure he was drunk.

We sat down to dinner and it was painful to watch him struggling awkwardly with his knife and fork, the handles of which he placed, using his right hand, between the disobedient and clumsy fingers of his left. As he ate, bits of what he was chewing fell from his half-open mouth back onto his plate. I noticed that because of his drooping lips, he was constantly showing some of his teeth. It looked as if he was growling.

'Do you remember how we used to go to the seaside every year?' I asked.

'To Vlahošane?' said my mother.

'Yes, we never went anywhere else.'

'That got fucked up as well,' said my father angrily. 'When the company went bust, they sold everything, the chalets, the land, everything! I then heard that our director bought it all for peanuts, demolished everything and built a hotel. Can you imagine? You run something into the ground so that you can then buy it cheap, like some fucking vulture.'

'I wanted to ask something else ... Do you remember Bobby?' I asked him.

'Who?'

'The little dog that we had at the seaside.'

'Oh, yes. He was a funny one.'

'How could we just leave him by the roadside? Who knows what happened to him then ...'

'What happened? Nothing good, I can guarantee it!' my father growled and clumsily wiped away the saliva that had begun to run from the corner of his mouth. 'Probably died of hunger in that rocky wilderness. Or some car ran into him on the road. Maybe a wolf or a jackal choked the life out of him. You choose which scenario you prefer!'

'But why did we just leave him?' I didn't want to give up.

'Why, why?! I felt sorry for him! The whole time I intended to take him into the bushes and hang him from some tree. I even had the washing line ready in the boot. Then I felt sorry for the little cur and I said fuck it, let him go where he wants. But I didn't do him any favours, believe me. He probably managed for a couple of days or weeks ... You see what happens if a man isn't a man, but a wimp.'

I said nothing more. With difficulty, I chewed and swallowed what I had in my mouth and pushed my plate towards the centre of the table.

'Aren't you having any more?' my mother asked

'No, I stopped for a hamburger when I was driving,' I lied.

'I've changed the sheets in your room and there are fresh towels in the cupboard. How long are you thinking of staying?'

'Not long, I've got to get back in two or three days,' in a moment I changed my original plan, and added by way of explanation: 'Monika and I are getting divorced.'

That was the first time I'd even mentioned her. Neither of them had asked about her. And now they didn't seem surprised or curious about what had gone wrong.

'She never seemed the right one for you,' said my mother casually.

'I'm going to the bakery in the morning, do you want anything special for breakfast? They've got croissants, poppy seed rolls ...'

I said I didn't mind and that I'd like to go and rest after my drive.

In my room, I first opened the window. I noticed that the house opposite had a new roof and a freshly plastered façade. The curtains were also new. Perhaps the neighbours were new, as well.

I lay on my back and stared at the ceiling with its brown wooden panels. Simply out of habit, I reached into my trousers and tried to masturbate, as I had done here, on this same bed, so many times as a teenager. But I couldn't concentrate, and when my wrist began to hurt I gave up. I thought that I no longer had enough of the required imagination. I sniffed my hand, which smelled of sweaty genitals. I should go and wash, but I couldn't be bothered to go to the bathroom. From the floor below came the muffled sound of dishes being washed.

I looked at the black bin bags and cardboard boxes of various sizes that were piled on top of each other all around the room, so that only a narrow corridor was left, from the door to the bed and the window. On some boxes it was written in capital letters what was in them: 'CLOTHES', 'TOYS', 'VHS CASSETTES', 'GLASSES' ...

But on most boxes nothing was written. I wondered whether one of them contained that length of blue washing line that my father had ready in the boot, that distant summer thirty years ago.

Translated by Maja Višenjak Limon

Ana Svetel

Osti on Mount Everest

The main bus station of the medium-sized Slovene town was flooded with secondary schoolkids, drinking coffee, smoking and talking over each other, squashed together at the tables of the shabby buffet, from which, far too early in the day, unbearable sound pollution was pouring. A little to one side sat Lena Malovrh, watching them and asking herself whether she had also belonged to such a tribe in her schooldays. She was tasting early adulthood with great pleasure, and whenever she came across a group of schoolkids she felt unlimited relief that that period in her life was past. 'I'm waiting for a ride, so I'll be off any minute. And I don't have an umbrella, so I'm underneath the roof,' she said apologetically to the waitress, who nodded without interest and, on her way back to the counter, was already immersed once more in her phone. At that moment a blue hatchback drove up, turned on its hazard lights and stopped on the place reserved for taxis. Lena glanced at her watch; he's early, she thought, picked up her rucksack and went over to the car.

'Hi there. Ljubljana?'

In the car sat a woman who was leaning back and carefully tucking a blanket printed with Martians behind the seatbelt of a child who was mumbling something. It seemed as if the little boy hadn't even noticed Lena, as the woman straightened the bottom edge of the blanket that fell across the child's legs, turned to face forwards and looked at her. They studied each other for some moments.

'Yes,' said the driver eventually.

'Can I sit at the front?'

The woman looked the girl over and once again was silent for a moment.

'Yes, of course,' she replied.

Lena quickly got into the car, put her rucksack at her feet and made herself comfortable. When they drove off she asked: 'Is it just us?'

The woman looked at her questioningly and then nodded.

On the cloudy morning, they left the bus station and the schoolgirls with false nails far behind them and drove through the rush hour. The woman drove without talking and Lena turned round to the child, who had in the meantime stopped saying anything and was silently looking out of the window.

'Hi,' she said, 'I'm Lena. What's your name?'

The little one looked at her and grimaced slightly.

'Go on, tell her,' said the boy's mother.

He said some name beginning with W but had his hand stuffed in his mouth so that Lena couldn't understand him.

'Rožle,' said the woman. 'He's a bit shy.'

'Hi, Rožle, nice to meet you,' replied Lena, still turned to face him.

'And this is Osti,' said Rožle.

'Who's Osti?' asked Lena.

'Here,' said the child, flapping his right hand.

Lena Malovrh smiled. 'Pleased to meet you, Osti,' she said, finally turning to face the front.

'Pretty busy at this time, isn't it?'

'Yes, it is, nothing's moving,' said the woman.

Lena examined her surreptitiously. There was nothing striking about her. She was one of those women who even in a baggy jumper and her roots showing don't look untidy, but merely relaxed. She joined the motorway and looked at the child in the rear-view mirror.

'Would you like a drink?'

'Juice.'

'Osti can have juice, there's water for you,' she said, feeling for the bottle of water between the seats with her right hand. 'There, have a drink.'

The boy unscrewed the top and drank.

'Do you go to school yet?'

'Going to see auntie Maša.'

'And who's auntie Maša?'

'Osti's going as well.'

'That's great.'

The woman did not join in the conversation, and so Lena once more turned to face the front and stared at the road.

'Do you often drive to Ljubljana?'

'We go when we have to,' she said. 'Quite often, recently.'

Lena looked around the orderly car, the bottle of water for her and Rožle, and in a Tupperware container on the back seat there was something that looked like an extremely healthy salad; the air freshener wasn't one of those smelly Christmas trees you get free from the insurance company, but a small, wooden ball smelling of cinnamon and cardamom. She watched the driver, who was without make-up, in profile: the barely noticeable down on her top lip and her firm chin. Lena wished she was an adult, driving in a hatchback to see auntie Maša, making her own air freshener for the car. She wanted to go into the woman's kitchen, peep into her bathroom cupboards, she wanted to know how it felt to be self-confident and ordinary.

'This rain's really awful.'

'Yes, it is,' replied the woman.

'Evidently in Ljubljana it's just cloudy.'

'That, at least,' said the driver.

Once again there was silence.

'Do you work in Ljubljana?'

'No, for days like this my boss is very helpful, he lets me use up overtime.'

'That's nice.'

The woman sighed: 'Yes, something at least,' and was again wreathed in silence.

'Do you like playing with your friends?' Lena turned round once again.

The little boy looked at her for a moment, and then he began to tug at his seatbelt and poke his fingers into the blanket.

'You know, the other day Osti went on Mount Evwest and stood on one foot on top.'

'No, that's brilliant!' exclaimed Lena, 'that Osti is a clever one. Did you go with him?'

'I waited with auntie Maša.'

'Your son is so cute,' said Lena to the woman and smiled.

Rožle's mother again looked at the little boy in the rear-view mirror and said without smiling: 'My brave little boy.'

Lena looked at the woman's shiny fingernails, cut short. Her left hand held the steering wheel in a practised way, her right hand resting on the gearstick. Then for a moment Lena glanced at the remnants of black nail varnish that still clung to her own fingernails in impossible patches and wiped her always sweaty palms on her jeans. She wanted to have the life of the woman sitting beside her.

'And it's so nice of you, offering ride shares. Few people with kids ...'

This time, the woman removed her eyes from the motorway and looked at her passenger: 'What did you say?'

Lena blushed: 'Oh, nothing, it's just ... it's not often I get a ride share with a little kid. I didn't mean anything by it.'

The woman put on the indicator and turned towards the capital. 'I still don't understand.'

'It's nice that you're on ride sharing,' said Lena, blushing even more. I do everything wrong, she thought.

'What ride sharing?'

'Sorry?'

'What ride sharing are you talking about? I'm not on anything.'

'Did you ...?' It suddenly struck Lena. She pulled her mobile phone out of her rucksack. Three unanswered calls. Two texts: *I'm waiting at the bus station.* And: NEXT TIME SAY IF YOU'RE NOT COMING.

'Oh god,' she said. 'I'm ... This is a mistake. I'm really ...'

The woman looked at her. Lena was as red as a beetroot. The woman felt sorry for her. 'Look, it's no problem. In a way it was quite brave of you to ask like that if I was going to Ljubljana.'

'But I thought you ...'

'Osti needs wee-wee,' came a voice from the back seat.

'We'll soon be there, love,' said his mother. 'Can Osti wait?'

'Hm,' said Rožle and began chattering again.

'I'm ... I'm so ...' stammered Lena.

'It's really nothing,' the woman interrupted her. She turned into a side street. 'Really,' she said again, somewhat quieter, 'it's nothing.'

The driver spotted an empty parking space and skilfully manoeuvred the car against the curb. Lena was full of admiration. She even liked the small cross shining on her wrist. The woman got out and helped her son out of the car, while Lena looked in her rucksack for her purse.

'Oh, forget about the money, really. As I said,' murmured the woman as she fastened the buttons on Rožle's little jacket, 'it was quite brave of you ... Anyway, we're a bit late. Rožle, wave bye-bye.'

Rožle raised his tiny hand and squeezed it twice into a fist.

'Bye-bye, Rožle, bye-bye, Osti,' said Lena, watching the woman's bouncing ponytail. She was holding her son by the hand and saying something to him. Lena stood between the tightly parked cars and watched them disappear into the large white building of the children's hospital.

Translated by David Limon

Uroš Prah

Too much light, of course
but nor is
the answer
to dim.

A lie, that the light's
too much
on the edge
of Văcărești
on the warm
concrete slope
the sun falls
chill
dreadgrove
when you were little
before
on seventeen
nightly incursion
you forced yourself inside
until it became
familiar even in the dark
even if this place
is not forest is not park
then what is it?
a failed reservoir

history pulverized
sunk into a semi-marsh
congealed to a half-savannah
they call it: delta
officially a reserve
what of?
'interventions' let's say
birds
and some guys, perhaps
cruising.

Prime places are those
where you should've
recognised what had been there
but didn't
the recent horror is no longer felt
this place strangely familiar
the compositions of its undergrowth
its few paths and even fewer structures
you strip off your shirt on the concrete
and expose yourself to the late sun.

Often in cities
I find myself in those green
wildest patches where
moving through reeds I think of
that night when above all we
slept your hard week away
in the morning you

sucked me of: I see
your choice to do
all that underpaid
communicative work
is in line with your
character of course
you're fond of your
own image who isn't
but above all: you need to give
actually it's something else
I wanted dammit once more
standing in the reeds in this
or that city
on a warm sunny
day in September
October maybe May
I seek – no, I find myself
I said I find myself
on a small path
which temptingly sways
into a thicket promising
home
distance
peace
some animal
a clearing
rocks
and right then for a moment I
remember your cock-filled mouth
I crawl towards this
that or the other viewing point

somewhere on the edge of the park
protected area a bit further down the coast
I stumble
stumble often upon the first guy
who's nervously turning about
then two more usually older
pious maybe sometimes poor
more often businessmen gays
still choose the most beautiful spots
they resist time embrace
each other they are like these
places themselves are
these places at once nervous
and calm lying in wait they
lovingly hunt only
consenting prey
bucolic scenes almost
drowned out by the heavy
traffic on the road just metres
away at a safe remove
above the family life on
the well-kept paths around the lake
marsh pond river
scenes of strolling gentlemen
coming to the hill from early
lunches or their offices or cardboard
mats down by the water they tamp down
these elegantly interwoven paths
sit topless on a folding
chair in the middle of a small meadow
they remind me of

where I come from showing
off the fact that my own body bristles
under the rustling of the reeds
tightens up beneath this sun
piercing the sparse foliage
it contracts in water
diffuses
with the dry dusty
dirt.

This melancholy strength
you can see it on my body
my domination
there is growth in protein
and across it info-streams
guilt networks.

When soil slides
ice is exposed to air
gas escapes

is it Batagaika that gasps and groans
or does something gasp and groan within it?
what might have been a mere scratch in the crust
what used to be a small clearing for a bit of road
began to slide and
this was no 'mere slippage'
this is a rockfall gushing stronger by the hour
popping strangely banging grunting
whizzing and whistling

here the underworld literally opens
erosion washing away all the earth
only gravel and rock remain.

The fish are black inside
our coast also breaking away
Carthage still falling
I don't know what tomorrow brings
the desert already creeps in
God is great
tight is the belt
of habitability
we're the ones who deliver them at sea
not those who leave.

Waves of warmth hammer
the shoulders of those waiting on the beach.

The withdrawn sea

Translated by Lawrence Schimel with the author

Katja Zakrajšek

Between 'Them' and 'Us'

I once accepted the Up-Goer Five challenge to describe my job using only the 'ten hundred' most frequent words in English. As it turned out, not only 'translate' but even 'language' were out, so I ended up with something like 'I read books by people who do not speak like me and write them again so people who speak like me can read them'. I rather like that this simplified definition says something essential about literary translation: of course this is about words, but even more than about words, it is about people, about their (our) societies and cultures and perceptions of self and other. For who are these 'people who speak like me', who are the 'we' thus defined and who the 'they' that are to be translated into 'our' language? What is it of 'theirs' that gets to be translated and why and for whom among 'us', and who decides what's valuable and relevant anyway?

Which goes right to the heart of an even wider question: who gets to speak, who gets to have their story told? We're a storytelling species, we humans. Not only is this how we understand ourselves, each other and the world in which we live; narratives are how we mould and shape ourselves, each other and our societies. Who gets to be at the centre of the stories we tell and consume, whose stories are perceived to be representative, to have universal value and appeal, and whose to be a matter of specialised interest – all of this is central to our self-perception as individuals and as societies. And translation is how stories travel across languages in our shared world – in space, time, or both.

Fair warning: whenever I try to say something about literary translation, I'll probably end up talking about Life, the Social Universe, and Everything.

***

I was presenting a novel for teenagers to a roomful of teachers in Ljubljana and it was question time. A teacher carefully explained that he was worried about the book's readability and relatability for boys, given that all of its three protagonists were girls. In what was not exactly one of my more diplomatic moments, what came out of my mouth was: 'Welcome to the predominant reading experience for women and girls.'

Piglettes by Clémentine Beauvais is a gloriously funny and unashamedly tender book about self-image, bullying and pervasive social messaging on how girls and women should be – which would be enough in itself, but doesn't even begin to do justice to the wide range of social and political topics it touches on. I thoroughly enjoyed myself working on its rich and playful language ranging from teenage slang through modes of online communication to philosophy jokes and literary references. When *#3špehbombe* was assigned as reading material for a general knowledge competition for students aged 12 through 14, I thought it was an excellent choice: a fun and challenging read that offers much to discuss in a group setting. Yet all of that was being swept aside by a persistent unspoken assumption: men as relatable by default, women as special-interest exception.

There are different ways it plays out. One memorable instance was a fellow translator at a residency in Arles asking me about the book I was working on – as it happened, it was *Ladivine* by Marie Ndiaye: 'What is it about? Is it about women? Because only a woman can truly understand the –' did he say 'womanly psyche' or was it 'psychology of Woman'? I forget. What I remember is the frustration. There is so much to say about Ndiaye's subtly observed, finely crafted and richly evocative prose, and about turning and stretching and weaving the long phrases she is famous for until their elaborate choreographies felt as airy and effortless in Slovenian as they did in French – hopefully anyway. But how do you get there when the starting point has just been defined as 'Is it about women?' Well, yes, it is, although I suspect not quite in the way the question was meant. It is telling that I've never had to answer the opposite question when translating a male author: 'Oh, you're translating a novel by Moacyr Scliar? What is it about? Is it about men?'

Despite all this, I soon came to doubt myself. Had my initial response been too sharp? Had it been a mistake extrapolating from my own experience as a young reader, a quarter century and more ago, since so much excellent children's and youth literature had been written in the meantime that has paid so much more attention to diversity and representation? Surely my own musings over how the male characters tended to get all the best and most exciting storylines and the female ones were either boring, annoying or both, no longer applied. (But they do, a friend would later inform me: her tween daughter has complained of the exact same problem in books she was assigned to read at school.) At any rate, the serious, well-meaning young teacher, confronted for what seemed to be the first time with the idea of discussing a book about girls with his mixed group of students, needed an answer in a short, usable format, and more to the point, his students deserved him getting such an answer. So after pointing out there actually were positive male characters in the book to relate to, I tried to explain that his male students didn't really need to be centred this way in everything they read. On the contrary, I said, there is real value in the experience of sometimes being relegated to the margin of a story if you're used to always being in its centre, and in trying to consider a different perspective. It's an exercise in imagination and empathy.

***

Obviously I've no experience of being a male reader, but I do have ample experience as a reader of books that pose a somewhat analogous challenge to the often invisible assumption of white European as default, everything else as special-interest exception. Comparing different ways your perspective might be denied centrality is a complicated task involving thinking about different types and axes of marginalisation. The discomfort this brings isn't necessarily a bad thing; it may simply be a natural reaction to being asked to step out of your own everyday shoes and enter a different sort of story showing your world in a light you're not used to seeing.

Literary translation, by definition, involves stories of 'others'. With all its imperfections and misunderstandings, it offers the possibility of reading the world in all its rich diversity in your own language: a gift. I am forever grateful that I grew up in a literary culture in which translation has never been an afterthought but rather a prominent part of our collective bookscape, and, historically, an immensely important factor in the development and consolidation of literary Slovenian. This meant that my socialisation as a reader was never separate from my socialisation as a reader of translations. I didn't have many opportunities to travel as a child and as a teenager, but I had my local library, and in neat rows on those shelves was the world. That, at least, was the idea. I would later realise that that world of mine was still only a partial one.

It is not just that, understandably, not everything can be translated to every single language (as a data point: Slovenian has

2.5 million native speakers). Nor is it simply a matter of, tautologically, feeling closer to neighbours than to more distant literatures. In fact, international literary relations are extremely unequal, subject to hierarchies of power and prestige that often have very little to do with literature itself and a great deal with the socio-political contexts it swims in. The Western literary canon may have long obscured this with its insistence that its only criterion was literary excellence, without considering how such judgements are themselves shaped by habits of thought and perception – including blind spots – we develop as members of our societies and people of our own time. The same logic that long held most women outside of the Western literary canon was also at work in excluding non-Euro-American writing, as well as establishing further hierarchies within that corpus of writing.

There is nothing abstract about these observations. When you look at what gets (or doesn't get) translated into a particular language – what publishers, translators and other literary actors choose as being interesting and valuable – what you see is an image of world literature shaped by this history. The specific results will vary somewhat from place to place and from time to time, but the translated corpus will always betray hierarchies of perceived importance. For a central language such as English it might be the case of preferentially translating from literary traditions that either seem important enough to be worth notice, or interestingly exotic. For smaller languages and their literary cultures, it might be a matter of identifying with the cool kids in class in order to fit in. I don't mean to say it is consciously planned that way, but the result of patterns of availability and visibility, of reading habits and assumptions of literary worth left unchallenged.

The literary map of the world as it exists in Slovenian is still largely focused on the West. While some publishers are intentionally

moving towards more inclusive programming, there is still a sense
that books by non-Western and minority authors need to work twice
as hard for half the consideration. This has even been my experience
in translating from English and French, where I tend to focus on
African and Afro-diasporic authors. Books in languages editors are
unlikely to be able to read themselves tend to fare even worse, and
those in non-European ones are at a particular disadvantage: it's
almost as if they don't exist until they are translated and noticed in
English. This roundabout route to existing in a third language even
seems to hold for writers such as my friend Saïd Khatibi, one of the
nominees for the 2020 IPAF (the so-called Arabic Booker), who
happens to live in Slovenia, but has as yet no translations into
Slovenian.

***

In the mid-2000s, when I was just starting out as a translator,
proposals for books by African writers were a rarity. I was often
asked why on earth I'd choose this unusual niche in a way I never
would have been asked about French or British writers (white ones,
at least). Attitudes have shifted since then, yet I still have a sense of
having to over-justify each proposal by pointing out how it single-
handedly fills a blank on the literary map where it still says 'Ubi
leones' – something that, as a rule, is not asked from books written
within mainstream Western literary traditions. These seem to come
with an immediate assumption of universal interest and relevance.
Nor are they usually burdened with representing an entire
community, country or even an entire continent. (This assumption
can play out in strange ways sometimes. Translating Congolese
writer Fiston Mwanza Mujila's experimental novel *Tram 83*, located
in a mining town in a fictional country in central Africa, was a

memorable experience for the ways literary form and language are taken apart and reinvented. What was also memorable was how one of the design suggestions for the cover, which I was fortunately able to veto, was a colourful image of Maasai beadwork.)

And how much representation is enough? I've noticed readers, even professional ones, are often quickly satisfied that they have read *a* book from a literature they know little about, especially from a minority one. (Additionally, instant relatability is required from this one book; as if the ability to gain something from a work of literature didn't grow with familiarity with the literary conversation happening around it, as well as with its larger historical and social context.) This certainly doesn't leave much room for multiple narratives to ward off the danger of 'a single story', to borrow the oft-quoted words of Chimamanda Ngozi Adichie, a wonderful writer whose books, paradoxically, are themselves in danger of being turned into 'single stories' for precisely this reason.

Some years ago, I proposed a memoir by Ngũgĩ Wa Thiong'o, *In the House of the Interpreter*. I had just translated the autobiography of Richard Dawkins for the same publisher. I'd jumped on that because I love good science writing. Not that I expected that a life (and its retelling) could be exclusively focused on science. But something I found jarring were the chapters dealing with the author's family history and his own childhood in the British Empire. At the same time, there were barely any other narratives of, say, colonial Kenya available in Slovenian outside of a grand total of two books about the history of Africa. So, in the spirit of correcting the omission, and because Ngũgĩ is barely known in Slovenian, and because *In the House of the Interpreter* is a masterful book deftly weaving personal story and collective history, full of lucid observation and luminous writing, I suggested translating it for a collection of life writing. The answer? Oh, perhaps I could try

Other Publisher; didn't they publish 'such authors'? How easily the British scientist's childhood perceptions of colonial Kenya had been accepted as an interesting and relevant part of an interesting and relevant life story. How easily the in-depth narrative and analysis of the great Kenyan writer and thinker were relegated to a literary ghetto.

***

For me, adding to the corpus of translated literature means inviting my readers to share my own wonder and exhilaration at exploring new works of literature, even whole new traditions of literature, and in the process challenging my own perception of what literature looks like, globally. It also means challenging the traditional Western canon, which I find stifling, unfair to both readers and authors, its long shadow still contributing to a lose-lose situation for both source and target literatures. I first became aware of this when I took a course in Francophone literatures at a summer school in Grenoble. I'd been studying French and Comparative Literature, considered myself well-read, but the authors I came to read that summer? I'd never even heard of most of them. The more I read, the more I was appalled that I had ignored whole literary continents, and more appalled that I had not even noticed that something was missing from my idea of world literature. There was one way of changing the restricted literary landscape I'd grown up with. I plunged right in.

By a monumental stroke of luck, I had my very first proposal accepted by the very first publisher. It was *Allah Is Not Obliged* by Ahmadou Kourouma, a challenging piece of writing interweaving standard European French with its African varieties and a smattering of pidgin for good measure – all the while commenting and insisting on their differences, as the child-soldier protagonist pores over the dictionaries that were his plunder. Looking back, I wince at my beginner's confidence. Yet somehow, judging from readers' comments over the years, it worked out.

Translating this novel was a crash course in dealing with the sort of inner complexity and diversity, tensions and hierarchies of power and prestige within a language that have no equivalent in Slovenian, a peripheral European language that was never the language of a colonial power. How do you even begin to open a space to represent such a linguistic constellation shaped by its history? It's a question I have kept asking, and trying out different approaches. Something I am certain of: grappling with such questions has larger implications than simply translating this or that book: it pushes at the limits of what can be said and thought in the target language.

***

I have just translated some poems from Persian. I don't know Persian at all. As a translator, you're emphatically not supposed to do that. But sometimes you have to.

It took me a lot longer than it should have to realise how many languages were being written right where I live. I had to look at other cities and their literary landscapes to notice this about Ljubljana, a city that perceives itself as even more homogeneous than it is, unable, as yet, to recognise its own multilingualism, steeped in assumptions about location and language that no longer hold true in the twenty-first century, if they ever did. This leaves writers in languages other than Slovenian virtually invisible as writers.

Add to that the lack of translators for many language pairs that involve a peripheral European language like Slovenian and/or a non-Western one like Persian. There may not even be the possibility of indirect translation where you work from a 'proper' literary translation in a third language. (Have you ever played the unfortunately named game of Chinese whispers? Indirect translation is a bit like that, except that what unavoidably gets progressively distorted is artistic effect rather than message.) What may seem like a very abstract problem as long as the literature thus left inaccessible is conveniently located far away, or perceived to be so, becomes suddenly urgent and frustrating when it appears at your doorstep. There are two poets in Ljubljana – that I know of – who write in Persian, and, it appears, no Persian–Slovenian translators at all.

When the choice is between breaking the invisibility and breaking the rules, sometimes you break the rules. Fortunately, the author can be an amazing translation resource. So we sat down together. We talked about the poems and their contexts, compared English versions the poets had themselves produced for the purpose. I asked detailed questions about particular words and lines. I even used Google Translate, may Saint Jerome forgive me. We talked some more. I looked at the originals that I couldn't read, but I could notice patterns of repetition that made me ask about effects of sound and rhythm. It's a strange way of reading, one I doubt would work with a longer text, let alone a novel. I wasn't even certain it would work for their relatively short poems, but what was there to lose?

Somewhere along the way, the opacity separating my language and theirs seemed to recede until poems emerged. No doubt their texts are tentative, uncertain, filling the gaps in comprehension I didn't notice with assumptions I wasn't aware of, creating other gaps for readers to fill in – and yet, there are meaning and feeling and beauty that have come through, somehow, speaking out to a new audience. We have just presented them publicly for the first time, reading in both Persian and Slovenian. There is a sense you get when the audience responds to what is read and you know that you've done *something* right. A door was opened where your readers may not have even known there was a wall, the world expanding by a few lines of poetry.

Rather than ask what is 'lost' in translation, ask what is gained: all of this.

WALES

Eluned Gramich

Something beginning with

Menna kept a travel journal. A slim, pretty thing she'd spent an hour prevaricating over before buying. She did her best to write in the evenings, after her son and daughter-in-law had gone to bed, but she laboured over every sentence and soon gave up. It was difficult to write in the first person, I-this and I-that, writing herself into the centre of things. She'd only managed:

Munich, Bavaria
July 2018

She carried the notebook with her anyway, just in case.

***

'Next weekend we can go to Lake S. You'll love it, Menna. It's beautiful,' Jessica said over a breakfast of cheese, ham and bread. Menna's tights-clad knees touched her daughter-in-law's bare legs under the IKEA table.

'The last king of Bavaria drowned there,' her son added. 'Or was assassinated, no one knows for certain.'

Menna said, 'Oh dear.'

'Don't put her off, Tomas! We love the Lake S. We go every month at least. There's a great restaurant there, too. Italian–German style. I've booked us for lunch.'

Menna had never heard of this lake. It was famous, apparently, the way they both let the name roll off the tongue without translation or explanation. Sta-something? Sah-something? Menna didn't know what to think of this new 'we' either. Not that she disliked Jessica – quite the opposite. The 'we' only discomfited Menna when it referred to a shared landscape, a shared being-in-the-world, such as this S-something lake. Instinctively, combative thoughts went through her mind: *What lake? Tomos doesn't know about lakes. He doesn't like lakes. Tomos isn't interested in nature. He prefers the indoors, warm pubs in the evenings, or tea in front of the television.* Then, on seeing her son's mountain boots in the shoe cupboard, his new raincoat and waterproof gaiters, she was forced to admit her mistake. Tomos had been living in Munich for five years, married for three; he'd changed. That was fine. Just fine.

Only they kept happening, those discomfiting moments. Tomos and Jessica liked to eat out at restaurants where Tomos – *her* Tomos – knew the waiting staff by name. Tomos chose freshly made pasta, pickled cucumber and cabbage, sliced tomatoes and radishes dipped in salt, where the Tomos she knew – the Tomos of Ceredigion, West Wales – subsisted mainly on digestives and *bara-menyn*. Tomos read German menus effortlessly, drank beer from the large, trophy-like glasses, and left too-generous tips on silver platters. Colleagues stopped him in the street, because he worked at the Munich opera house as a scene mechanic and therefore was, apparently, quite well-known in this part of the city. Jessica worked in PR. Although what that entailed Menna still wasn't sure.

***

Later that evening, she was blindsided by an argument. They were side by side in the kitchen, she and Tomos, preparing supper. Tomos was shelling peas, his fingers slender and soft like hers. Jessica was chattering away on the phone in the background, and so Menna found herself chattering away too: small talk about what she'd observed so far in Munich. The cleanliness of the streets; the punctuality of the public transport.

'The trains aren't always on time,' Tomos interrupted.

'They're so fast though,' Menna said. 'And clean.'

He nodded; his newly tanned face bent over the bowl of discarded skins.

'Shame about the language, though. It's not the prettiest, is it?'

Tomos glanced at her. 'What do you mean?'

'All the "ch" sounds,' she said.

He stopped what he was doing. 'For God's sake, Mam. There are "ch" sounds in Welsh.'

'I suppose,' she said, carefully. 'But it's not the same, is it? *Achtung*! and all that.'

She should never have said anything; should never have opened her mouth. *I didn't mean it like that*, she heard herself saying, but it was too late. There it was: Tomos' frustration, his disappointment with his mother. She was a sheep, swallowing wartime propaganda, duped by old-time villains in Indiana Jones and James Bond into believing national stereotypes. A xenophobe. Uneducated. He didn't say the last two, but she knew they were there, hovering behind his tongue.

But she really didn't mean anything by it! It was just something you said. It didn't *mean* anything. It didn't mean she disliked Jessica, or the south-German city, or his new clothes, his Italianate sandals. It was all lovely, really, she wanted to tell him. I love you, she wanted to say. I don't know why I said it. Or, more truthfully, I don't know why you're so angry with me. You never used to be.

'Don't be annoyed with me now, Tomos,' she said instead. 'No need to snap at everything I say.'

'I'm not snapping,' he replied, more gently, regretting his outburst. 'I'm pointing out.'

It was the spectre of the past, she thought, as she silently peeled potatoes. The spectre of Paris. The last time she'd been abroad, they – Menna, her husband, Tomos' father – had visited Tomos while he was completing an internship at a French theatre company. How she'd hated it. Her husband wasn't well, and she'd been worried. What if they had to go to hospital? What if they misplaced his tablets? What if the food didn't agree with him and it triggered the vomiting again? Everything posed a danger – the cars seemed louder, faster, more toxic in Paris than in London. The shops more claustrophobic. The people stiff and uncaring, even the language they spoke seemed purposefully designed to cause her panic: fast, unrelenting, completely impenetrable. Tomos, so in love with his freedom, his urbanity, insisted on taking them around one historical wonder after another, and all she wanted to do was take her husband back to the hotel. A cup of tea with milk. Bed.

It was a long time ago now – over a decade. Now her son was thirty-five and her husband had been dead for almost four years.

They finished preparing the meal in silence; then, as she laid the table, Tomos came to her and said, 'I'm happy you're here. I've missed you.'

'Oh, now,' she said, giving him a smile that hid how upset she was. 'Thank you for having me.'

***

Gorgeous sun. The sky a taut linen above her, light blue. Munich's central square all elegance, medieval towers, the warm onion spires of the cathedral, the tourist shops selling wood-carved figurines: red ladybirds, woodpeckers, pine martens, Alpine flowers. The windows dressed in white lace and the blue-white flag of Bavaria. Off, towards one side, there was the market her son had told her about. The market beginning with V. She was so hungry. They'd left for work early. Jessica said *Help yourself* only there was nothing to help herself *to* – half an inch of milk and dry-looking muesli. It was one o'clock at the square beginning with M. There were visitors here, like herself, who kept close to the town hall, cameras pointed upwards, waiting for the famous bells to chime. Menna had admired enough historical monuments; it was time to eat.

V-something was a semi-permanent market of small counters and stalls. A beer garden stood at its centre, and surrounding it were bars with white stools and high round tables where people were served a bright orange drink in bulbous glasses. The bakeries subsisted of walls of dark-brown breads, plaited and studded with salt. Wheels of cheese, baskets of fruits: cherries, strawberries, blueberries, like gemstones glittering, portioned out into blue-white paper cones. A row of butchers sent head-spinning smells of roasted beef and grilled sausages into the afternoon, followed by the salty aroma of fried bacon. Doughnuts in icing sugar. Broth ladled out into two-handed ceramic bowls.

Menna wandered, getting hungrier and hungrier. She was too nervous to approach the more popular stalls. There were no queues, just people clamouring for their orders at random. She walked until she reached the far end of the market square where, on the corner, there was a kind of walk-in bakery with a few tables and chairs. A man in his early sixties – around Menna's own age – was eating a cheese sandwich. A cheese sandwich: now there was a goal that, in this ocean of newness, Menna felt she could achieve.

The server spoke, but Menna didn't know what was said. There seemed to be no English menu, or menu at all, and no clear way of obtaining the sandwich the man was eating at the window. The server addressed her again, a little impatiently Menna thought, and a familiar heat rose to her cheeks. People waited behind her. At this point no words, English or otherwise, were going to leave her mouth. She desperately looked for something to point at – a pretzel would do, the thick crusty ones her son ate with his beer. 'That please!' The server followed her finger to the wrong bread. 'No, no,' she said, until she gave up out of embarrassment.

'Yes, thank you.'

Are you sure? The server seemed to say, waving the enormous dark loaf Menna did not want. 'Yes thank you. Thank you.' Menna put ten euros on the plastic platter and stared at her hands. She ended up at McDonalds, telling the story of the failed lunch to herself in a way that would make Tomos laugh rather than feel sorry for her.

***

Still. Still ... It was not like Paris. As long as she didn't have to communicate in any way, Menna was content. In fact, when walking the Munich streets, Menna felt a lightness in her being that she hadn't felt in a long time. It reminded her of the first months of marriage. They'd rented a flat above a laundrette: she worked at the town archives and he worked at the garage. A time before their son, where they came and went as they pleased, and the world seemed open and free, just how she wanted it.

Tomos worked until five and Jessica until six, which meant one whole hour with her only child each day. She met him at the fountain in the central square – he wore thick workmen's trousers with a white shirt and his hands were often spattered with paint, but he insisted on taking her to the famous delicatessen to buy ingredients for dinner. 'Look, Mam. Do you see? They've got real live lobster in the water here. Do you want one?' She shook her head, peering at the grey-translucent beings in their blissful ignorance.

White sausages in their skin. Sweet mustard. 'You have to drink beer with it Mam otherwise it's no good.'

'I've got something for you,' she said, taking out the enormous loaf she'd purchased by accident. She told the story and they both laughed, but neither of them cut the bread for dinner.

'Farmer's bread it's called,' Jessica explained. 'It's hard as rock. We don't usually buy it. You've got to really chew it down.'

She put the loaf in the kitchen and Menna never saw it again.

***

Menna walked everywhere because she was too afraid to take the tram. Her son had given her a ticket, but she didn't use it, fearing an inspector would come and accost her in German. The situation seemed very real to her, an excruciating possibility: a uniformed inspector threatening her with a fine and she none the wiser while the rest of the tram judged her for her ignorance ... In any case, walking was good exercise; although, she thought, it would be nice to go further afield. To the N-something palace Tomos had mentioned, which was so crowded at the weekends but quiet in the weekdays. Three days left, yet still she had not managed to visit the palace. She didn't dare suggest that Tomos take a day off work; he was extremely busy. It was the summer festival at the opera and so, during the long days Menna was left on her own.

'You're welcome to stay longer,' Jessica said in the few hours they had together in the evenings.

'Thank you, bach,' said Menna, certain then that she would not.

***

On the underground with Tomos, a canvas bag on his shoulder with that night's treats. Menna was offered a seat, so she took it and peered up at her handsome son, who was now old and young at the same time. She never thought she would be the mother of a thirty-five-year-old, but there he was – strands of grey in his charcoal hair, stubble along his jaw. How much like his father he looked; more so now, with his eyes closed; the green-blue eyes he'd inherited from her. His head resting against the pole; another long day behind him. There was grease above his left eye she wanted to wipe away. Behind her young-old son, she saw an advert written entirely in English:

SALE NOW ON
German summer courses
SPEAK LIKE A PRO

At dinner, Jessica and Tomos looked at each other across the foldable table. The look was private, heavy with shared knowledge. For a second Menna thought they were about to tell her to leave. They had discussed it, and they preferred it if she went to the airport a day early because they'd had enough. But instead Tomos said, 'Mam, we've waited for the right time to tell you. In person, like. You're going to be a Mamgu.'

'Oh goodness.'

'Due in September,' Jessica said. 'A boy.'

'Really? Oh! How wonderful!'

Panic took hold of her. A grandson! But he would grow up here, far away, a different child to the Welsh children she knew, the Welsh child she'd raised. 'Lovely,' she said. They took her reticence for shock and overwhelming love. They showed her the scans, updated her on the midwife, the blood tests. All well. Here is his elbow; here his nose. Menna could not eat anymore; there was a knot at the bottom of her throat she couldn't swallow away. At night, on the sofa bed, she didn't sleep for imagining her future loneliness, her grandmaternal lovesickness.

Oh, now, she cried to her husband. *Would you have guessed that this would finally happen? A babi on the way, and you, cariad, not here to meet him.*

They'd waited to tell her in person, because she was far away. Her grandson had been alive in his mother's belly for seven months without her knowledge. She was far away – in another country, another language, a foreign way of being. It was not her son or daughter-in-law that were foreign, but her. Menna. She balled up the sheet in her hands and cried.

It was always going to be like this, she thought, over and over, until she gave up on sleep and took out her phone. Then, somewhere before dawn, she opened her son's laptop.

***

On her last full day in Munich, Tomos and Jessica took her to Lake S. The silhouette of the Alps stood on the other side of the water, no taller, it seemed, than an oak tree, traced into the sky. The lake itself was large, spinning into the horizon. It was impossible to see the whole or have a sense of its contours and shape. It was easy to imagine a king dying here, overlooked by mountains.

Wooden piers jutted into the lake here and there, and it was on one of these that Jessica laid down their picnic things. There were reeds in the water; the water itself was so clear Menna could make out the colour of the grit, the pebbles and stone – black, red, grey and white. It was cold: the icy water of the Alps.

'I've got something to tell you,' she said.

'Are you pregnant too?' Tomos asked. He was lolling happily on his towel, dripping after a short swim. Jessica lay with her head on his thigh, smiling up at them both.

'I've decided to stay a little longer,' Menna went on.

'Good!' Jessica said, quickly.

'But not with you. I know you don't have much space. I've rented a bedsit a few streets away.'

'There's no need to rent a place. Stay with us. We don't mind.'

'I want to be here when the little one comes.'

There was a hesitation then; Menna felt it. 'Don't worry. I don't want to come to the birth if you don't want me there. I don't want to be ... to be *busneslyd*. I can't think of the English word now.'

'Nosy, pushy ...' Tomos translated, even though she'd never spoken to him in Welsh when he was small.

'Yes. I don't want to be pushy, but I want to be in the same country at least, so I could help if you wanted. I'll be in the background, only here if you need me, I promise. I know your parents live in another city Jessica.'

She nodded. 'It won't be easy,' Menna found herself saying. 'A baby isn't always easy.'

'No,' said Tomos, but she knew that he couldn't understand what she was talking about.

'And I'm going to learn German,' Menna added. 'I've registered for this course at the university for something to do. I'm probably a lost cause.'

The young couple smiled; Menna noted that they did not disagree.

***

The language school was an old, narrow apartment block in the university quarter of Munich. Six floors with no elevator; each floor a different language level. Menna was on the ground floor. They tried to make her sit a test, but she explained that the only German word she knew outside of *Danke* was *Essen* – food – which she'd learnt from her son, calling them to dinner in the evenings.

Ten students in the class, sitting in a horseshoe shape around the room. The blinds on the window were twisted and lopsided. Menna had a new file, lined paper, highlighters and pens in a leather pencil case. She was the oldest student in the class. The others had sleek gadgets propped up in front of them, or else just a phone in their hands.

She tried to guess each nationality before the introductions; she was wrong on all counts. There was Daniel (Spanish), Clarissa (Italian), Samuel (Israeli), Deborah (Tanzanian), Martin (Italian–Swiss), Maya (Hungarian), Jonas (Brazilian), Chiara (a second Italian), Erik (Czech). Frau Riedel, a forty-something-year-old teacher, skinny in black denim, talked very quickly and copiously in German. The teacher didn't seem to expect anyone to understand her monologues; it seemed more to herself that she muttered, rapidly and somewhat nervously, as she gathered the materials of the day and distributed the photocopies. To signal the start of the lesson, Frau Riedel clapped her hands and said, 'Gut! Dann.'

Good. Then.

Gradually, Menna filled her lined-paper and folder with her language work. It was a surprise to her that she didn't flounder immediately or, indeed, give up on the course. She hadn't counted on how simple it was – writing down the words she didn't know; repeating the words her teacher uttered; covering, over and over, the same roleplays with her classmates. *Ich heiße Menna und ich komme aus Wales. Wie heißt du?*

In fact, it was surprising to her how difficult it was for others: she found herself filling the sentences her classmates could not complete or correcting their mistakes. At times, Frau Riedel deliberately didn't ask her to read a text, because she knew Menna would read it well: better than the usual 'Englishwomen', Frau Riedel confided in her at the end of one lesson, whose monolingualism made it impossible for them to pronounce vowels openly.

On Friday, the end of her first week, the Brazilian Jonas suggested they go to the beer garden. Students from the higher floors of the language school – the fluents and the intermediates – were also heading to the Chinese Tower in the central park. The arrangements were made in English – the language that everyone spoke, more or less. The young people congregated in the cramped courtyard at the back of the school, smoking and drinking vending-machine coffee. Menna headed to her little flat, where she had leftovers from the night before – pea soup and rye bread. Jonas called to her, 'Where are you going?'

'Home,' she said.

'You're not coming? No?' he asked. 'But we are all going.'

She laughed. 'I'm too old.'

Jonas didn't laugh; instead, he looked at her with bewilderment, as if he'd never heard such an excuse before in his life. 'Fine. I'll come for one drink, but I can't stay long.'

'Good,' he said, matter-of-factly, as though there could be no other answer.

***

She stayed until midnight. She stayed until the spun lights of the beer garden shone like fireflies between the chestnut trees, and the band on the higher floors of the Chinese Tower slowed their Waltz and Polka playing, and there was nothing left but the cool night air and the clatter of beer glasses and the hum of mosquitoes and the long, woozy walk home through the park, between a student from Italy and another from Brazil, their stories joining and blending with the countless tales and half-tales she'd already heard that evening.

'Do you know Daniel? He is in your class. I think what we have is something special. Do you know I have been with my boyfriend for a long time, almost two years, and it is not the same as what I feel for Daniel. I know he has been with others at the school, but he says with me it's different, and I feel it too. You understand?'

Menna nodded. 'He's a nice boy,' she said to the petite Italian girl whose arm was linked with hers and whose breath smelt of sweet prosecco she'd preferred to beer.

'He's nice, yes. He's going to come and visit me in Turin.'

'Is he now?'

But Menna was not sure, suddenly, who Daniel was – the Spaniard? Or the Brazilian? In the long night, she had spoken to so many people, their names blurring into one name, yet their stories had been so different, running through her like the beer she had drunk ... Too much beer, too many tales. The Brazilian on her right: he was telling her the reason he was learning German. He came from a part of Brazil, the southernmost part, where there were many German descendants and they also had Oktoberfests and spoke still in the dialect of German their ancestors spoke, in his case, Bavarian, has she heard real Bavarian, it is almost indiscernible ...

Then there was Erik who was going to make a film about his home town, that is an industrial city north of Czech Republic, no, it is likely you will not have heard of it, Erik is a fan of David Lynch, he will be the David Lynch of the Czech Republic, he has a camera here, with him at all times, much better than a phone camera, look, take a look at the photographs he has taken surreptitiously of their teacher in her black mourning clothes ...

Her parents have died and that is why she wears black, Deborah knows, she understands German better than any of them, she has lived here for years, she is married to a German and soon she will have his child but not yet, she's waiting for the certificate, at home, in Dar es Salaam, her brother has died and the funeral is that day, the same day, but she cannot join because of the visa, she has three brothers but this one was her closest, her dearest brother because there was only eighteen months between them, Tanzania is the most beautiful and most peaceful country in

Germany I will set up a beauty salon, there are many special creams and products in Hungary and I'm talented with hair and hair-style, it's my speciality, so I will set up a salon here, maybe in the east of Munich, but first I have to have better German, once, when I was a child, I was a model here, I walked the catwalks and modelled clothes in Maximilianstrasse, Armani, MaxMara, Dolce & Gabbana

In the autumn I will go walking in the alps, to Italy and Switzerland, by myself, I draw and sketch, I have experience of climbing mountains, crampons and ropes, I will go up the Matterhorn, but I have heard terrible stories, once, while I was staying in an Alm hut on the slopes of such-and-such I heard a man had died that same day because a small stone had fallen and hit him directly between the eyes

You will be a grandmother? A Großmutter? An avó? I am so close to my own grandmother. She is everything to me. We write postcards to each other and she tells me how best to live

***

When she arrived home in the early hours, she took out her travel diary and wrote:

Under the chestnut trees, glass flagons of beer. Sparkling gold. Jewelled wasps, coming to take a bite. The smell of roast pork attracts them. It's nothing for you, cariad. You and your allergies. Did you know ... In Brazil, they drink a green herby tea called maté (ma-chee) out of an earthen cup. In Switzerland, it's important to speak French and German to get ahead. Everybody has heard of Prague, but no one has heard of Ostrava. At least, I hadn't. There are more people in Budapest than the rest of Hungary. There are better cakes in Hungary than Austria. Here I must try the Bienenstich, the bee sting, and the Prinzregententorte, the cake made in honour of the Prinz Luitpold. I must eat it in a café named after him where there are fountains, mirrors and rude waiters. I wish you could come with me, cariad, but I shall think of you when I take my first bite ...

Menna went to sleep with ink on her hands, having forgotten to eat her leftovers.

***

The restaurant is the first test of a language-learner. Menna invited her son and daughter-in-law to the German pub, the Augustiner. They sat in a Bavarian *Stube*, a warm room of dark wood and vermilion floor tiles, and the Herr Gott's Winkel – the lord's corner – where a crucified Christ hung suspended above Menna's head.

'I'll order,' Menna said. Then, faltering slightly, 'I'll try to anyway.'

But she ordered, and it came. They talked about work, and Menna talked about her classmates, always-in-black Frau Riedel, Friday nights at the Chinesische Turm. 'I know how to say the German name for it now,' she said.

'Sehr gut!' Jessica said, kindly. 'There's a saying *Deutsche Sprache, schwere Sprache*. German language, hard language.'

'Yes, love. I think I've heard it said.' Strange, how Menna had not noticed her daughter-in-law's bulging stomach until the end of the first week. Jessica was not a slight woman and, thinking about it, she'd worn work-like smocks and billowing maxi dresses, and drank – although Menna couldn't understand the different labels at that time – *Alkoholfreies*: alcohol-free beer that looked identical to the alcoholic variety. And yet Menna was embarrassed at her own failure to see the most basic changes in her daughter-in-law.

Jessica turned to Tomos. 'Willst du noch länger bleiben? Musst du noch wieder in die Arbeit?'

'Weiss noch nicht.'

'Don't feel you have to stay,' Menna said quickly. 'I know you're busy, bach.'

'We can't hide anything from you now, Mam, can we?' Tomos said, touching her arm. 'I'm alright to stay for a bit. I only have to be there in the evening now.'

Menna tried to explain what was happening to her: how the city was slowly beginning to open up; how each new word she learnt seemed to draw back the curtain on a new scene; each point of grammar introduced a new act; each conversation, a new character. Gradually, more and more of this German play was making sense to her, and she could see, too, how in time she might leave the audience altogether and alight onto the stage herself.

Instead, she said: 'I finally managed to buy a 12-stripe ticket for the tram and underground.'

Tomos smiled. 'Now you've just got to use it.'

***

In the travel diary, she wrote:

There are four art galleries: one for old paintings, one for not-quite-so-old, one for modern and one for radically new. In the latter there are things you wouldn't like, cariad. A statue of a woman with a baby on her stomach, still attached by its umbilical cord. The woman is looking at the baby in surprise, as if saying How did you get there? And What am I meant to do with you now? I think of Jessica and the little one. I worry she won't let me help, even when she needs it. She's independent, like I was with Tomos ... I didn't ask for anyone's help, remember? I did it all by myself. You at the garage and me at home minding the little one. You wouldn't like the art galleries, cariad, and I'm not sure you'd like all the travelling, the here and there of it. But the beer you'd like, isn't it cariad? The beer and Tomos' company ...

***

Frau Riedel asked about their weekend plans. It went around the class, and everyone answered with *nicht viel*, not much, until it was Menna's turn. 'I'm going to the palace,' she said. 'The one beginning with N.' This was received as an invitation, and all ten of her classmates met her at the central tram stop the next morning.

Menna found herself sightseeing with company for once. A troop of young people, who spoke in a mixture of German and English and who, for some reason, accepted her uncomplicatedly, as though the four decades separating them was nothing in comparison to the goal that united them: learning to speak in another tongue.

The sun stung, as the German saying goes, so Menna bought a parasol from a street seller and strolled around the symmetrical gardens of the N-something palace. No, not the N-something. *Schloß Nymphenburg.* She walked the white gravel paths, circling the perfect lawns like green handkerchiefs. The young classmates took photographs with their phones: she posed with them, ate with them on the palace steps. Still, she was glad when she could eventually break away, meander through the marble rooms, trace the rope with her fingers, scan the signs in German and in English, her eyes matching the two languages to each other. Around her the opulence and luxuries of another Royal family and all she remembered was the German word *Kachelofen* for the tall, ceramic stoves, and the tongue-twister that meant marble hall: *Steinerner Saal*.

Near the bedrooms, a group of German children in matching yellow caps appeared, giggling excitedly over one particular room. Menna waited for them to go ahead of her, one friendship bubble after another, laughing and whispering. When at last she was able to enter the room, she realised the reason for their hilarity was a nineteenth-century toilet.

She laughed herself, and when the next little group of children came to have a look, she turned and said to them, *'Ja, ja. Sehr lustig!'* Very funny! And smiled even more, thinking about the daftness of children – *Kinder*. She would be entering into that world soon, where she would learn a new language: the language of silliness and wonder.

Steven Hitchins

Ynysfach

       subtery metalicon crustre
       gurglimpses of flushingdark
water tunnels hollows bores through stains rocks orange
solar debris rains
       esoteric ether
       crystalline spiralling
I put two grams iron in water
following night I'm face to a big grey wolf in dream

Leaving Parliament Lock the canal enters a manmade moonscape.
Dandelion McDonalds cup trench between cindertips. Midway
through hills of cinder, berghaus fleece walks tiny dog, says alright
butt. High stone bridge arches over skateboard car park. Smaller
arch a narrow gauge tramway from Ynysfach works.

       twenty pound a month
       fifty-two weeks in a year
       unless it falls on christmas day
       only day she shuts is christmas day
       what about easter then
       no she's open easter

Canal curves south-west towards Rhydycar ironbridge. Fly lands on
my canvas bag and rubs its feet together. Soily smell trickle-plips.

At Rhydycar ironbridge the boat turns southerly and passes under lattice span of Brecon & Merthyr Railway, and expansive elliptical arch of Vale of Neath. Birds creak and chudder. Puddle shudders twig reflections.

dark mood low energy nigredo all day
 haemal hemisphere
 tectonic solutions
first cells lipid bubbles on mineral surface
 fission stars
 stellated of primordial tonic
 sidereal siderite
the wolf alchemically speaking stibnite

Aberfan

When daylight comes there are no hymns. People scuffle through classrooms, one looking for dawn. Smoke pours down at small panes collapsing above us. Fog so thick we can barely see each other. Last time I would see many of them. I hear a rumbling and look outside. Mr Williams shouts.

Birdcheep brambles. Net window dog yip. Gustled bouquet of dead TV aerials. I don't like anything else. Recycling sacks flail billowfull. Bus breezes the corner. Every time it's the same person. Hedge blooms and exhaust. Cigarette logo on sleeve-swirled window. Maroon hive skewered with bun-pins. Stubble heads sweat. Stop saying it shut up. I was like oh.

Wreath visited almost everybody. The tailor sews his last black tie. Chapel lights wink. Breath of white chrysanthemums in front room. I run out and see a man's legs sticking out of the ground. I try to pull but someone shouts and water pours down I think he must have drowned. Somewhere in the mud lies a girl's shoe. I think she's alive but a man says it's no use. My leg hurts but I manage to pull it away from the shoe.

Stream plaits sky. Ladybird bag stuffed litterbin. Trolley parked in gravel lane. Deli club triangle box. Oh my god I was just about to say that. Frays of Pepsi logo quail from roadsqueezed litre flask. That fucking thing no let's not go there. Purpley brunette leatherlegs propped against bus shelter. He didn't do anything this time no he was just standing there. Pylon over rooftops. Huge boys in shorts clamber into tiny Corsa. Keys tinkle engines wheeze.

A crash and I'm lifted, carried across the room still at my desk. Knot of window. Eyes open then water. Man rubs dust from trousers of glass. Smoke hands. Woman on front wall cradles baby. Miner in hardhat holds steaming papercup. Breath mists, hands on hips. Flashbulbed policemen. 11 am I hear the newscast. Put my helmet, spade, torch, gumboots, oilskins in back of the VW. Tell Olwen I'm driving to Wales.

Abercynon

Bonal sheepstone, aboulder ropen. Rave us moons. Jaw barge clostle regrow. At the bottom of the Elevens the canal turns south-east, chewing over bargees flaring icicles. Under the railway incline, over the aqueduct, over the Taff.

On, on in a nectar of clanghammers. As we draw near platforms, shovels to the mountain slide past explosions. Ledges drip bluebells and a snipe nest above us drips silver in the shovels.

Navvies scarecrowed over icebreakers, iron and clear, as we slide. The trees I saw beyond heard their hanging on a shriek of tobacco. Flannel shirts open to the moon. Silver to the death. Soapy arms sweating over frozen land.

We watch unspeaking as a barge slides past. Bargees nod briefly, brown and bulging. The great railway washtub in a window-shriek of sweating houses as we swing past above them, loading gloom, on down all twink.

Take her slow, my father calls. Furnacemen wind-bright from the prow, fire and neck-ties. The navvies straighten with knives of tram, muck-red to the whisper as we pass. And the lads glowing in the trees nod dusk in the stones.

Rhydyfelin

Clatterations. Hushes through intermetallic vegetation. Powdery insect blacksilver. Tin-mill west bank of Taff opposite Dyffryn. Wooden picnic tables. Rugby club buddleia gravel lot. Anyone fancy a mooch round down there?

Intricate stingies. River cartooning quartz through liquid flutter. Fire buckets hang from rafters. Battered paintflaking sign. Rhydyfelin RFC car park. Cars left at owners' risk. Long rods of tinbar sheafed against wall. I am a few others may well be up for a smooch around.

Dark morph under tin works rust scrawls. Figures dip the metal plates. The hollow faces. Sharp iron thin into rolling crimson. Well then, enough chit chat why don't we get a group of us together this coming Saturday and head on over there? Shaft attack via pallet yard plant-flames. Steel draincovers in tarmac. Blue metal container. Pleochroic skims.

*

Clang landscapes. Pigeon hoot translucent. I first visited the tunnel when I was about 8. I recall wearing wellies and I could feel the ground. Train hushes through trees behind rust girder roof.

Intermetallic gravel. I rub the lime from the plates after they have been polished. Have done for six months. Forked steel palisades. Long brick rectangle buildings. Liquid hammer hall. Rust skeleton jungles.

Shearers cut packs. Openers split sheets with hangar. Picklers clean them in bubbling acid bath. The lime gets in my eyes and makes them sore. I work from six in the morning until six and sometimes eight at night. My earnings are 6s 8d a week. Lustre picklers. Belching mesh. Crosshatch prismatic. Battered warehouse sky.

Nantgarw

14 lbs of China clay
18 lbs Lynn Sand
14 lbs Bone
13 ½ lbs Felspar
12 ½ China stone
11 ½ Flint
110 Borax

Stipple calyx. Petal ions. Whole surface florid. I must now tell you Father has got into a situation. When the lock is filled and I've made level I put the towline back on the mast. Open the gate and get the horse going again. JCB croaks backwards out of hatch. Bristly shrubs. Scrubgrass and buddleia lot through barbed mesh. Lanky ragwort. The agent's house and warehouse opposite the pottery, Edward Edmund's boat dock and the brook feeding the mill. Moss-fringed pavements. Leaves whisper. Cracked polystyrene tray by dandelion clock. The brook supplies water through a succession of holding ponds. Stream culverted under canal. Hubcap banking. Heol Crochendy.

14 Smart Solar Ltd
15 Timpson Ltd
16 Castle Court Funeral Home Ltd
WESTBANK
B1a Greggs (shop)
B2 GB-Sol/EETS@Renewable Energy Works
B9 Invacare
B13b WW Truck & Bus
B15 Invacare

Pearlicious tiptoe vibrates a surface of petals. Ivory sepals fold a colour lens. I had some thoughts of writing to him, but hardly knew how to act, as his conduct was so strange. Private parking these barriers are locked at end of each day. Magpies on buttercup daisy lawn. Black glass office perimeter. Storehouse on the wharf. Lorries behind steel palisades. Under the bridge the canal loops past the grounds of Dyffryn Ffrwd and passes Graig Cottages. Homes of colliers who worked the levels of Craig yr Allt. Always liable to flooding when river is high. Heol Pardoe. Redbrick blocks. Vertical blinds. Plastic wrapped pallets behind lorry doors. Wasps buzz in broom bush. Wippen the melodious clay. Calcinate the bone marriage. I wish I had means to send for you – I have none.

Melingriffith

Stalked rotor. Cyan snag of purr. Lichen gloss gurgling from sulphuric stratum. Tickly snakescale leaf-wift on gulp sun.

Outer geomantic fringe of the M4/A479 interchange. Shrouded metallurgical centre, in manorial records the mill is not named.

Scrackled cracture. Tinfoil faces tinker brittle. Oxide tickle of ingot icecubes.

References occur to 'myne', marl, wood, 'coles' and limestone, and also to 'sows' and 'washed iron'. We follow the line of power saws.

Splash canopy. Scuffle fronds. Dark-dropped crink
high in pirouette. Bites of blistered chirpsong.

> *If you want Maddock you may keep him as we have as*
> *many colliers as we can find houses for.*

Crackling cascade. Tinge water of boiling casket.
Stagnant melts.

Cardiff

A visitor enters Cardiff from the east, under railway bridge into
Crockherbtown. Hardhats in sunglasses talk and point, leaning on
shovels. Smell of tar, hum of digger. Seagulled glut on drift digged
pluggets. Quartz canal a sedimentary remembrance. Ah knackered.

As we walk west from City Road the felspars are closely packed.
Crockherbtown widens: houses metamorphose in submarine ridge
settings. Strongly veined lavas interspersed with a handful of shops.
Going to the game tomorrow? Sort tickets for us. Remnants of
ophiolites in tectonic situations: a few schools and the Theatre
Royal.

*

St David's arcade is brought to the city from the carboniferous beds
of Hydrequent. Hands in pockets, ears plugged in. Eyes glaze numb
from chill-smacked faces. Canal flows through lime-mud pillars
between shops and shallow lagoons. Plinths of sky.

Outside the Pastimes shop a thick black line traces the wall towards East Gate. Recrystallization fills cavities with undulose layers while calcite invades others. Waves pound, break up and regroup the sediments. Fountains and plant-beds are travertine conglomerato.

*

Southern part of city a thick cover of recent drift. She said please don't and I said alright well I'm just there I'm just there for a good time ain't I. The letter is stilted and alleys rattle. Out on the marshlands buildings stand on drift deposits. Siliceous terraces like stands of tar.

On the boulevard of dryness, the season limbs defiant. Squirrel silhouette scampers across slinks of trees. Leaves sunlit like stained lavas. Coral crushedral. Veins jargon. Heeled boots clop across Esso forecourt.

Sea lock

Ruins of ancient hoodie courtyards. Steelchair verandas halfmoon out above. High walls of church and alley blot out moon. Onions squished amid fallen sycamore propellers. Men sit on car bonnets. For a moment I can't see even a glim.

      wrinkled winds
  lockwaters swept in ripple-knit croak
     whistles pricked
        thatchen wriggings

A light shines ahead and the lane opens into a small yard. Herring gulls bleat-wheeze. Caged fans buzz. Faint banging of the sea grinding out of freezing wares. Another raucous burst from streets at the mallard-moorhen border. I feel myself along the wall.

*

I unhook up and paw the rickety plain. Swamp burns on backs of uniform arms. Bean wigwam yards. Gull guffaws over washing-lines. Polka drapes whirr on aerotrail verandas. Polystyrene tray cracked in argent puddles.

> pulse wellings
> wavelvets
> plume-wriggly gurgle-cluck skies
> tuft-smudges runchen
> lunchy thud
> scoot-nibble

Tiger leans burst from cirrus handful of gulls. High walls squat on the shadows between walkways. The quays bask like slugs. Outside lamp above door. I walk towards it and see my overnight case on the step. I tug it and whirligig. I unhook the shadows.

Lloyd Markham

Locked in/Loose screw

A creative mistranslation of Aljösa Toplak's
'Into the realm of square circles'

As Vladimir Rebolov pulls the child by its wrist, the others bow their heads. The nearer they come to the hole at the end of the hallway, the more the child tugs back. It peers up at the onlookers – hoping to see some small ember of sympathy in their coal-dark eyes. There is none. Their faces are empty. Their hands tap robotically on portable screens. As always.

The child cries.

Vladimir stops – strikes.

The child falls, then scrambles up, tries to flee. The others restrain it. When Vladimir grabs it by the wrist again, it gives in and follows.

It is easier to make out the interior of the hole now. There is the outline of a chair angled up towards a ceiling of metal and glass. When the child sees the belts hanging to each side of the chair, it freezes. Vladimir drags it forward.

He lifts up the child. 'In we go?' he asks someone, then places the child into the chair and pulls the belts tightly around its chest.

'Can you breathe?'

The child shakes its head.

'Liar.'

Vladimir points to a dot on the ceiling. 'What do you do when this one lights up?'

The child points to a button behind the chair.

'What about this one?'

The child shakes its head.

'Exactly, you do nothing.' Vladimir points to the ceiling again. 'And this one?'

The child points to another button. Vladimir slaps its hand.

'Wrong!'

The child looks around – points to a handle beside the chair.

'Come on now. Remember it already.' Something pulls Vladimir's attention back to the hallway behind them. 'What? Yes, of course he will,' he answers some muffled voices. When he returns he is holding a helmet with a pitch-black visor. He shoves it down onto the child's head. The child squirms as its ears are folded – squashed by the tight rim of the helmet as it slams into place and seals.

'Be steady,' says a muffled voice. 'Behave.'

The child's world goes dark. It holds its breath. Its ears slowly unfurl in the cramped helmet – the world unmutes by a fraction. The black visor lifts and the child can see the wrinkled hawkish face of Vladimir again.

'I will close the door now.' He scowls. 'Do you hear me? Count to a hundred. You can do that, right?'

The child stares.

'Count to twenty and then do it all over again five times, alright?' He shuts the door – submerging the tiny room in darkness. There is the metallic screech of a lock slowly grinding into position. It rings in the child's ears before fading into silence – leaving only a heavy, laboured rasping. The child soon realises this horrid sound is its own breathing. Then, just as its eyes adjust to the near-black, harsh lights cut through the eigengrau as buttons and screens and indicators flicker to life. Pain. The child winces. Its vision adjusts. Then the handle beside the chair blinks blue and begins to vibrate.

The chair shakes.

The whole room shakes.

The child closes its eyes. Breathe in. Breathe out. Deeper. Deeper. Deeper. The buttons start to blink faster and make garbled incomprehensible sounds. The speakers crackle.

'... me? Can ... me? Pre ... button. Over,' says a voice.

The child presses a button on the ceiling.

'Got it. It's underway. Over.'

The room trembles. Steel groans. Alarms scream. Air is sucked from child's lungs.

Silence.

Then the ominous cling of something small and metallic hitting the floor behind the chair. Horror flutters in the child's stomach. It turns in its seat – or at least turns as much as the belts will allow – and searches for the origin of the sound. The floor is unlit. It can't see anything. It tries to run its hand along the surface of the floor, but can't quite reach.

'Core is being heated. Fuel, four minutes. Over.'

Several buttons blink. The child presses the button next to the chair.

'Central,' crackles the speaker. 'Everything is in order. Over.'

It presses the button again.

'Central. We are confirming that everything is in order. Over.'

'Listen to them,' says Vladimir's voice. 'Everything is in order. Over.'

The room quakes. The child feels like its bones are being shaken apart.

'Core is being heated. Fuel, three minutes. Over.'

The child presses the button again.

'Central,' says Vladimir's voice. 'He's just panicking. Everything is in order. Over.'

'Central. Confirmed. Over,' says the other voice.

'Side motors are now active. Over,' interjects a new voice.

The child clings to the seat, breathes steady and slow – stifles the tears. It again reaches behind the chair.

Fingers wiggle uselessly in the dark.

The room shakes. The child braces. Its heart thrashes. There is a fresh ringing in its skull. Its gritted teeth rattle. Louder and louder. The blinking buttons become smeared rays of light. The walls are crumbling.

Silence.

One of the lights squeaks.

'Core active. Over.'

'Fuel. Two minutes. Over.'

Letting out a sigh that is almost a whimper, the child again stretches, again catches nothing. It just can't reach far enough. It looks at the belts restraining it.

'All side motors active. Over.'

The child tugs at the iron clasp on the belt. It does not move.

'T-1, leave the tower. Over.'

The child punches the clasp. Nothing.

'Level 2 problems with fuel flow. Over.'

'Central, confirm the status. Core? Over.'

The child punches again with all its strength. Little splits form in its gloves. Its knuckles sting. The clasp releases. The child quickly crouches, runs its hands along the floor – scanning, searching.

'Core is active. Over.'

'Fuel, one minute. Over.'

The child catches a solid particle in its glove. A fallen screw. It glints.

'Countdown in two minutes. Over.'

'T-1 is evacuated. Over.'

The child looks toward the ceiling – tries to spot where the screw fits.

'Fuel emission terminated. Over.'

The room trembles. The child is thrown from its seat. The screw slips from its grip as it is hurled towards the wall – helmet smashing into a light. Cracked glass catches the surrounding radiance – flickering like distant stars. The child hugs the chair and waits . . .

A couple of buttons beep.

'Motors ready. Over.'

'Fuel successful. Launch in two minutes. Over.'

The child climbs down from the chair and once again searches for the loose screw – running its hands along every surface, probing every corner – but it just can't find it. It presses the button.

'Central, everything is in order. No one is there anymore. The tower has been evacuated. Get ready for the launch. Over.'

It presses the button again. When there is no answer – it presses again. And again.

The child starts punching the button. Plastic caves into metal. Blood pools in the index finger of its right glove. Stinging fades into a dull ache.

'Countdown in a minute. Over.'

The child bites its lip. On all fours it sweeps its hands over the floor one last time.

The screw is nowhere.

Some buttons buzz.

'Get ready for countdown. Over.'

'Side motor starting. Over.'

The child weeps. It slaps the ground in frustration and climbs into the chair.

'Confirmed. Launch in one minute. Over.'

As it sits down, something stabs its thigh.

The screw is on the seat.

'Core starting. Over.'

The child grabs the screw, looks up at the ceiling. It feels around for some recess. The room begins to shake once more. The child holds on to the chair with one hand, reaches upward. Pained grinding metallic roars. The noise hurts its ears. The room shakes faster and faster. Lights smear into jagged lines.

Then it finds the little hole in the ceiling. It carefully puts the screw inside and turns.

It fits.

'Thirty seconds.'

'Son. Can you hear me?' asks Vladimir.

The child grabs the belts.

The room lurches.

It drops them.

'Son. You won't be able to hear us for a while, alright?'

The child again grabs for the belts. The bolts holding them in place rattle off their fixtures. They come apart in its hands.

Then the screw comes loose again and falls to the floor.

And then another. And another.

'It won't hurt. It will shake a lot and you won't be able to breathe so well, but it won't hurt. You're a man, you got this!'

The child doesn't know what a 'Man' is.

'Initiating countdown.'

'The view up there. I've heard it's very nice.'

The child punches the button. Kicks the speaker.

'Ten, nine, eight . . .'

'We will cure you, son.'

It kicks again. The speaker crumples.

It hugs the chair. Its head hurts.

Everything is shaking, shaking, shaking.

The noise is unbearable.

The lights are unbearable.

Then something pushes the child into the seat.

Its fast laboured breathing stops.

Pressure in the eyes.

Chills along the back.

Then, suddenly, it is in a place where the sights and sounds no longer hurt.

Morgan Owen

Broom on Mljet

One part Blodeuwedd
and a glimmer of colour
on a dry slope.
A vestige of Wales's dream
on the sun's old soil.

Broad-leafed anemone

Since I first found you
you are trusty
co-travellers.
You follow the sun
from your recesses,
rising as praise
from the rocks.
In the shell
of the old Roman palace,
we stare together
through the breach in the wall.

A parachutist in the leaf litter

Did he fall? He hangs
by a leg
a straw's breadth
above the tree's
first dead;
summer is in retreat
and the battle about to turn.

Eavesdropping
in his cage
of air
on the plans of the soil,
his comrade
in the world's unfurling.

Riverside

Belly to belly you lay with the captured river,
demure and silent.
The crowds trooped past
with their arms full of waste,
tears, one-night wildness,
chance love and long stares,
though no one saw your face.
The men on the top came to celebrate your burial,
but did not see that the grave
was green.

Once calmed, you raised a hand
of summer's last flowers
and in your gentle gesture
disclosed
that a city's strength
can stitch all dispersals
with our scattered roots.

Alder

I lie with the alder's roots,
a piece of wood,
sediment-in-waiting
in the ebb and flow
of this river.

The indestructible

tapping their fingers
on a skull here,
a root there,
listening to the flow
of rain
through the moss
and the caves
which widen
with each blink

of the old
slow eyes
of time.

The tawny owl

An open window against the stifling summer
and the dust of an old room;

Aberystwyth murmurs
under the dead weight of night.

A mumble arrives on the breeze
between me and the darkness,

a glimmer of sound
like footsteps in the air.

Then the sound's sketch shattered:
a tawny owl's clear call,

sliced through the dead canvas.
I was rooted by her song

in summer's swell the dead of night
as strong as a house's grasp

on the hill's empty page.

Dogroses

My flowers in the scorn
of lost places,
a lantern brighter
than pollution.
On the breath of the waters
carry me
to the needles of love
arm in arm
with the budding city.

Skull

The moon wears
a skull
and bears
a fistful
of aqueous silver
to adorn
the still shadows
of a dead house.

Translated by Nici Beech

Grug Muse

Weeping

I broke my heart once
and I wept
until my swollen, salty eyes
turned into two fat toads
and jumped into a nearby ditch.

And seeing this,
my tears turned into fish,
bright sticklebacks
and salmons, that dived
one by one into the sea.

Some turned into snowflakes
that buried the kitchen floor
in deep drifts
up to my thighs.

Some turned into shooting stars
and shot through the window
like the tears of San Lorenzo,
in red sodium chloride flames.

They turned into owls
with bilberry eyes, that flew

into the trees to hunt
for field mice.

I coughed white moths
like tears from the bottom of the chest cavity,
who went to chew the wool jumpers
in the bedroom cupboards.

And I wept until strange sounds
rose from my belly,
beating against my ribs,
plummeting through my lungs,
and I spat tears of sunflower seeds,
which fell on good soil
and grew, and flowered
into long-necked yellow
magnificent blooms.

River glass

I draw them one by one
from the riverbed. Some as small
as seeds, some with prickly
angles, the shape of buttons
or domino pieces.

While getting milk on the way home
they fall on the counter
like coins from my purse.

A little dirty,
the river mud coats them,
dulling the blue and white.

I find the smallest ones
in the seams of my pockets, I scrape
them out under my nails
and place them in jars
in windows
to swim in the sunlight.

Raw wounds of the shattering
licked by the grey tongue of the river
and smoothed again into whole pieces.

lost

monday i inform them that i'm missing i fill the appropriate
paperwork note my height [in my heels] the colour of my eyes
[cold] my weight [less than it's been]

they search the usual places ditches the backs of taxis slate quarries
my face appears on postboxes and on streetlights

i practise my silence noiselessly place forks on plates glue felt to the
soles of my shoes wear clothes the same colour as the walls

i eat rice and meat and my face is orange and swollen under the
electric lights of the takeaway no one recognises me i pay in cash

and there are no dishes to be washed i learn to still my ribs while breathing the skin of my face begins to peel from the postboxes

they get in touch to tell me that the case has been put aside give me a unique crime number a helpline [8.00–18.00] leave the taxi drivers be

it rains and then dries again i learn to float without water to walk without touching the floor

i wake up in an empty house on an unfamiliar morning i get dressed i open all the windows

Horizon

(South Beach, Aberystwyth)

Things gather in estuaries.
Tides come and go, and flotsam collects.

And last night's drunks wake up on the beach
and trip towards home
as the early dog-walkers
the lycra-and-porridge-joggers
and the fruit-juice-yogis start their day.

Last night, the bodies of
jellyfish came to the shore,
a shipwrecked navy

of rosy transparent mounds,
wet kisses on the gravel.

And the smoke still rises, white-blue
from last night's driftwood fires.
And plum-eyed students
in slippers, pyjamas with polystyrene coffee come
to immerse their toes in the water.

And the sea is as blue as a lie,
cold as a bread knife,
rubbing small stones into smaller crumbs.

Tonight, again, things will gather
in the estuary, bits of wood and plastic balls
and seabirds. And new drunks will come
to light new fires and join each other
under messy blankets, to share fragile secrets
like eggshells. Their gaze
on some long and far
off line.

cartography

these are the maps that lead the tips of my fingers to distant places
along field borders and back roads and the small squares of houses

and I also have my favourite scars
beneath my toe at the base of my spine
the tip of my finger

the empty corners of [nothing here] the [Managed Access]
and [danger area] places that the map cannot contain

their raw wounds quarries and reservoirs
fig and pomegranate places
and all the lost names

Translated by the author

Rebecca Thomas

Crib notes on the Dragon's Back

It starts with a name. An unremarkable name at that. Our plan is to escape to the Mynyddoedd Duon. This is Wales's most easterly mountain range, and not to be confused with Mynydd Du, which stands guard between Sir Gâr and Powys. No, these mountains peer towards a different border. As geographical happenchance would have it, one summit is claimed both by St George and the Red Dragon. Twyn Llech is England's highest mountain south of Yorkshire. Its Welsh neighbours laugh on – and down.

There are three summits on our list, a horseshoe on the map. Waun Fach lies at the centre. The responsibility that comes with being the parent peak has left its trace on this mountain. Although technically higher in metres, it doesn't stand as tall as its south-eastern infant, Pen y Gadair Fawr. A chimney once marked its summit, but this has long sunk into the earth – a cause of confusion for walkers seeking the highest point; disappointment for those after a photo to prove their achievement. Mynydd Llysiau stands to the south-west, facing Pen y Gadair Fawr across the valley yet ignoring its brother completely. Although the shortest of the three, this mountain suffers no inferiority complex. It shuns height, taking pride instead in its long and narrow ridge.

Our plan is to extend the horseshoe into a – nearly – circular route: car park > Mynydd Llysiau > Waun Fach > Pen y Gadair Fawr > Waun Fach > car park. But escaping is no mean feat. Roadworks ... a SatNav with a mind of its own ... more roadworks

... the mistaken assumption that we know better than the SatNav ... Escape is not so appealing when the timetable lies in tatters. After depositing the car in a pub car park – an important detail to which we'll return – there is not a second to spare. We are seeking the perfect marriage of endorphins and self-satisfaction: the ecstasy of exercise and ticking off each mountain on our list.

Seven hundred metres above sea level, a change occurs. Haste is not welcome here. The red kite is in no hurry, a generous bird whose flight facilitates the perfect picture. The sheep are in no hurry: this is their path they'll have you know! The breeze is in no hurry, knowing full well that it has several hours yet to coax my hat to its grip. We are in no hurry either. Although allegedly smart, a 'pause' button enables me to deceive the watch on my wrist. We can take several breaks with no negative impact on our 'stats'. Olympians, we are not.

Seven hundred metres above sea level, the two motorbikes are in a hurry. They scatter the red kite and the sheep with their roar and pollute the breeze with their smoke. Escaping is no mean feat.

Seven hundred metres above sea level, the greetings can be counted on a single hand. Despite the blue sky, despite the time of year – a weekend during the Easter holidays – you won't find Pen y Fan's traffic here. Summiting South Wales's second highest mountain is not such a laudable achievement. Most go in search of the additional 75 metres. One *morning* on the path up Mynydd Llysiau, *hello* twice along the ridge to Waun Fach, and a *would you like me to take a photo* on the summit. One finds a unique friendship in the mountains. The fresh air breeds contentment, contentment that breeds a desire to offer strangers a helping hand.

Our *helo* is different, of course. A simple *o* rather than *oh*. And *plis*, not *please*, to the offer of a photo. Nobody notices. Not the older pair in their matching raincoats, not the group of lost school pupils searching for a Duke of Edinburgh award, not the athlete who strides up the mountain without bre aking a sweat. Certainly not the man attempting to connect with otherworldly beings – or enthusiasts on nearby peaks – through his radio set. His sights are set on bigger things. But we have reason to pat ourselves on the back. Through our brave pronunciation of vowels, we are playing a part in a revolution. Perhaps we'll be brave enough to venture a *bore da* ('good morning') next time.

Having reached the final stage of our – almost – circular route, we turn to Y Grib, a ridge connecting the mountain to the car park which avoids the boredom of retracing one's steps. This side of Waun Fach is more popular for some reason, a long line of people like ants in the distance. Although more numerous, the greetings are short. *Hello, hi* ... Those fighting their way up have less breath to spare than those flying down.

There is a need for care here. The landscape is constantly shifting – grass turning to rocks before turning to grass again. For a while, there is no real path. We encounter instead a series of half-paths, the marks of heavy-footed individuals – or sheep – attempting to lure us to follow. We have quite a bit of experience with such paths: paths that tend to disappear underneath your feet. But the way forward on Y Grib is clear enough too. Follow the ridge downwards, falling then levelling, falling then levelling. After reaching the bottom there is an opportunity for the more energetic walker to venture upwards once more. This is the smallest climb in the chain, but somehow the hillfort of Castell Dinas succeeds in casting a shadow over Y Grib itself.

I am not taking sufficient care, that's the opinion of one man coming in the opposite direction. He has a point, to be fair – I shouldn't be checking my phone. But the stranger's judgement grates. The unsolicited – and unnecessary? – advice goes beyond the unique friendship one finds in the mountains. I mask my irritation with a smile, and hope that the man goes on his way. But he has a story to share.

You haven't woken it have you? It moves sometimes you know.

O?

The Dragon!

Social anxiety required swallowing the story gratefully, laughing, and wishing the stranger a good day. But the dragon stayed to circle above our heads, its bulk blocking the sun, its wings agitating the wind. The dragon was Y Grib, I had understood that much. But the significance of the metaphor was lost on me. Was there something peculiarly draconian about Y Grib? Or is every one of Wales's mountains a dragon now? That's the opinion of the *Dragon's Back Race* (the Welsh *Ras Cefn y Ddraig* too, for those with keen eyesight), a multi-day race between the castles of Conwy and Cardiff (two national symbols for the price of one here), along 'the mountainous spine of Wales'. Every mountain a dragon, and a dragon every individual who conquers them. We climbers can take pride in our draconian identity.

Dach chi'n siarad Cymraeg? (Do you speak Welsh?) The dragon is forced to flee as we respond enthusiastically to the unexpected greeting from another young couple. About five hundred metres above sea level, there is no need to hurry. Time must be made for the necessary, customary question: *O le 'dach chi'n dod?* (Where do you come from?) Time must be taken to analyse the answer.

*

By now, we have ticked off every one of South Wales's mountains. From Twyn Llech to Moel Gornach, from Twmpa to Cefn yr Ystrad. Some more than once. Bannau Sir Gâr are particularly privileged to have a spot in the SatNav's 'favourites' list. The magic of these mountains can catch a walker unawares. There are no words qualified to describe them. There is no camera that can catch their true nature. This isn't simply an attempt to avoid the task at hand. If an objective pair of eyes stops to study the mountains sheltering the two lakes of Llyn y Fan Fawr and Llyn y Fan Fach, they will observe that the slopes are sharper, the ridges flatter, the colours greener. From the peaks, the sea is within sight, Somerset even on a clear day. But the real magic isn't visible. Here, I can be. Somewhere in the fog between Fan Hir and Fan Gyhirych, every 'thank you' becomes *diolch*.

Nothing compares with seeing a view for the first time, the unique perspective on a land gained from twirling on a peak. The view is always new, the perspective always unique. The mountain is never still, never familiar. But nothing compares either with hearing a familiar language in an unexpected place. We are far from Fan Gyhirych here. The dragon is sensible to flee.

We part ways with the couple and crest the wave of our excitement to the final stage of our journey: the ruined hillfort. Very little is known about Castell Dinas. A medieval castle, a temporary home for the Norman lords of the borderlands. Unfortunately, it left little impression on the written record. Probably a place where languages and cultures interacted. Likely the site of several battles. It would be an impressive capture for an army. It is hard enough for two walkers to stumble to the top.

But it has a longer history too, buried in the Iron Age. Here I am indebted to the archaeologists: we do not have the skills or expertise to interpret the ruins. It is they who hold the key to the past at Castell Dinas. And they have so many keys in their keeping. Where will the keys fall once the endless cuts have floored the keepers? The universities may save money but will lose something more. The ruins are silent today.

*

My mind has wandered to a dark place, and the dragon is not to blame. But on reaching the car park, the abstract dragon reappears, this time in a more concrete form. The Dragon's Back – not to be confused (as far as I know!) with the race. I hadn't paid much attention to the name of the pub on arrival – we were running late, after all. Now we have the opportunity to admire the dragon in all its glory. Was the pub named after Y Grib? Or was Y Grib named after the pub? Did the gorse have a particular taste for beer?

I was convinced that Google would have the answer; Google would confirm what I already knew from the OS map and my old walking book: the ridge we'd walked along was called Y Grib. But no, I click through page after page without a 'crib' in sight. 'The Dragon's Back' was the latest fashion, an attraction appearing in walking blogs from the 2010s before multiplying to supremacy within the search algorithm.

And so, we have another dragon. We've never been short of these creatures in Wales. They were not always so graceful as the creature on our national flag, mind. When Geoffrey of Monmouth turned his hand to shaping national myths in the twelfth century, there were *dracones* fighting underneath the land of Britain. It is the same creatures who are at it in the medieval tale of Lludd and Llefelys, Welsh *dreigeu* this time. And in poetry, many a medieval Welsh prince is called a *dragon* or *draig*. But if we venture a little further into the past, we find creatures of a very different nature in the Welsh mountains. The cleric who composed *Historia Brittonum* ('History of the Britons') in ninth-century Gwynedd had an interest in dragons too. But here they are called *vermes*. Snakes, serpents ... or worms. A worm isn't quite so appealing as a national symbol somehow.

But this new dragon in the Mynyddoedd Duon was more than just a placename. There is a mythology to entertain us too. This is an example of what Irish scholars call *dinnseanchas*: a story that explains a name. We've never wanted for these in Wales. Middle Welsh *ystyr* ('meaning') derives from Latin *historia*. The purpose of telling a history or a story is to explain. I'll turn to the second branch of the Mabinogi for an example. The Irish king, Matholwch, is visiting Britain when his horses are deliberately maimed. The king of Britain, Bendigeidfran, promises fresh horses, to make good for the insult. He gathers foals (*ebolion*) from one particular province, and thence the province is named *Tal Ebolion* ('Foal Payment'). There was no name too small or too large to be the subject of a story in the Middle Ages. The author of *Historia Brittonum* set about explaining the largest name of all: the Island of Britain. According to this story, an individual called Britto, a descendant of Aeneas of Troy, was the first to set foot in Britain. From his name, then, the island was named *Brittania*. Centuries later, Geoffrey of Monmouth added a further chapter. After the death of Britto (Brutus in this text), the island was divided between his three sons, Camber, Locrinus, and Albanactus. Thence *Cambria* (Wales), *Lloegr* (England), *Yr Alban* (Scotland).

The *dinnseanchas* for Y Grib is not so detailed. This new legend simply alerts us to the presence of a sleeping dragon in the Mynyddoedd Duon. We have several of these already in Wales. Indeed, the dragon on our national flag is fairly unique in being awake.

Let me return to the *vermes* in *Historia Brittonum*. Here we have the story of a battle between the red and white dragons set down for the first time. Gwrtheyrn, king of the Britons, has fled to Eryri. His intention is to build a fortress to defend himself from the English who are sweeping across the island. But otherworldly powers conspire to cause chaos. Gwrtheyrn collects all the necessary materials to build his castle, but every stone and piece of wood disappears overnight. Naturally, this happens three times. This is a staple for Welsh mythology: why do something once, when three times does the trick? Gwrtheyrn's wizards have a strange – and bloody – solution: the king must find a fatherless boy and sprinkle his blood on the castle's foundations. Fortunately, such a boy is to be found in Glywysing. Perhaps unsurprisingly, the boy, Emrys, is not keen on his part in the scheme. Instead, he convinces Gwrtheyrn to dig beneath the foundations of the castle. There, two dragons, two *vermes*, can be seen sleeping on a tent – one red, one white. Emrys and Gwrtheyrn watch as the dragons begin to fight. To begin with, the white dragon is on top. But in a development all too familiar to rugby fans, the red dragon finds its strength in the second half and defeats the enemy. It pushes the white dragon from the tent completely. In case Gwrtheyrn doesn't understand, Emrys offers a detailed analysis of the metaphor. The tent is your kingdom, he explains to the king. The red dragon represents your people. The white dragon represents the English. This is a prophecy that echoes across the Middle Ages and beyond.

Emrys does well from the meeting: Gwrtheyrn hands over the castle in Eryri. This is the *dinnseanchas* for the hillfort of Dinas Emrys near Beddgelert. Another iron age hillfort and a medieval castle of some sort. But it is the story of the dragon that has endured. There is a dragon-shaped bench, an opportunity for visitors to enjoy 'Merlin's pool' on the path up to the ruins ... The author of *Historia Brittonum* can be satisfied: his work has achieved undisputed impact.

Nearly 1200 years later, the dragon has found a new home. These creatures clearly have a soft spot for hillforts. But medieval stories always spoke of two dragons. Which one lies asleep in the Mynyddoedd Duon? And where has the other fled?

Translated by the author

Biographies

CROATIA

Marija Andrijašević (1984) is a poet and writer. In 2015 she received an MA in Comparative Literature and in Ethnology and Cultural Anthropology from the Faculty of Humanities and Social Sciences in Zagreb, and she attended a study programme held by the Centre for Women's Studies in Zagreb. She debuted with an award-winning poetry collection *Davide, svašta su mi radili* (David, they did all kinds of things to me, 2007). Her poetry has been translated into a number of European languages and included in multiple contemporary anthologies (*I u nebo i u niks, Hrvatska mlada lirika...*), as well as the Italian anthology of selected poetry from the Balkans, *Voci di donne della ex Jugoslavia*. In 2018 she received the yearly scholarship from the Ministry of Culture to write her first novel, *Zemlja bez sutona* (Land without sunset) which was published in 2021 and went on to win the regional Štefica Cvek award for one of nine best regional novels and the 15th tportal Literary Award for best Croatian novel.

Katja Grcić (1982) received an MA in English and German Language and Literature at the University of Zadar and an MA in dramaturgy from the Academy of Dramatic Arts in Zagreb. She writes poetry, prose, drama and essays. Her early poetry collection *Nosive konstrukcije* (Supporting constructions) was published by

Meandarmedia in 2015, followed by a bilingual edition of poetry and short prose *Ljeto/Summer* in 2017, and experimental prose *Pisma Ziti* (Letters to Zita) in 2020. Some of her poetry and drama was broadcast on the Croatian Radio. Her drama texts *Molekule* (Molecules, 2017), *Smrtopis/Prekinuta veza* (Obituary/Interrupted connection, 2018), *Strah tijela od poda* (The body's fear of the floor, 2019) are available at *drame.hr* and won several prizes. Her drama monologue *Proljeće naše zlovolje* (The spring of our discontent) premiered within the *Monovid -19* project at the ZKM theatre in Zagreb in 2020.

Maja Klarić (1985) graduated from the Faculty of Humanities and Social Sciences in Zagreb in English Language and Literature and Comparative Literature. She works as a literary translator, editor and cultural event organiser. She organises and leads the international poetry gathering *Wood Poets* in Istria. Her poetry has been published in all relevant Croatian literary magazines such as *Zarez*, *Quorum*, *Knjigomat*, *Poezija* and is included in various anthologies as well as in a school reader. She is a two-time recipient of the UNESCO/Aschberg scholarship for a writers' residency in Brazil. She has published the poetry collections *Život u ruksaku* (Life in a backpack, 2012), *Quinta Pitanga* (2013), *Nedovršeno stvaranje* (Unfinished creation, 2015), as well as the travel books *Vrijeme badema* (Almond time, 2016) and *Približavanje zore: Put 88 hramova* (Approaching dawn: the path of 88 temples, 2019). *Vrijeme badema* has also been made available as a radio novel and an audiobook, and is included in the catalogue of the Croatian Library for the Blind.

Dino Pešut (1990) has graduated from the Academy of Dramatic Art in Zagreb with a major in Dramaturgy focusing on drama and film writing. He works as a dramaturg and director in Croatia and abroad. As a playwright, he debuted with the play *Pritisci moje generacije* (The pressures of my generation) at the Croatian National Theatre in Split, and his next one, directed by Saša Božić, premiered at the Zagreb Youth Theatre in Zagreb. In 2016, he was invited to attend the programme *Stueckemarkt* as part of the festival *Theatertreffen* in Berlin and the play premiered in German-speaking countries at the Burgtheater in Vienna in 2019. He is the winner of five Marin Držić Awards which are granted by the Ministry of Culture for best new dramatic text. He writes the 'Futuring' column for the newspaper *Večernji list*. In 2018, he published his first novel *Poderana koljena* (Torn knees). He is currently developing and writing a new project – a book of literary coverages and poetic travel writings focused on ex-Yugoslavian capital cities.

Maja Ručević (1983) graduated from the Faculty of Humanities and Social Sciences in Zagreb with majors in Croatian and French. She works as a journalist and translator and is the winner of two poetry prizes. Her debut novel *Je suis Jednoruki* (Je suis One-armed, 2016) was shortlisted for several awards and tells the story of a disabled Sarajevo musician. Her work has been published online and in literary magazines. She is currently working on a new work of fiction. Her translations from French into Croatian include Adeline Dieudonné's novel *La vraie vie*, Laetitia Colombani's novel *La tresse*, and Gilles Legardinier's *Completement cramé*, all published by Znanje press.

GREECE

Iakovos Anyfantakis (1983) moved to Athens for his studies, and eventually completed a PhD in contemporary history, focusing on the memory of the Greek civil war in literature. He has published three books of fiction: the novella Αλεπούδες στην πλαγιά (Foxes on the hillside, 2013) that was shortlisted for a national young writers' book award, the short story collection Ομορφοι έρωτες (Beautiful loves, 2017), and the novel Κάποιοι άλλοι (Somebody else, 2019) which received the *Reader* magazine award as the novel of the year. His books and short stories have been or are being translated in more than five languages across Europe.

Filia Kanellopoulou (1991) studied Philosophy at the University of Athens and Acting at Delos Drama School and is currently a postgraduate student in drama, performance and education at the University of Athens. She has published the poetry collection *Ta mesa mou* (My inner world, 2019) which won the Jean Moréas New Poet Award and was shortlisted for the Giannis Varveris debut poetry award of the Hellenic Authors' Society. Her first play *Women – Maybe Not – Alone in the City, July at 40 C*, was staged in June 2018 at Tempus Verum Theatre in Athens. She is currently working on her second poetry collection and preparing her first play for publication in the form of a graphic novel, in addition to experimenting with screenwriting and directing short films. She works as a theatre teacher and actress.

Dimitris Karakitsos (1979) studied at the School of Business and Economics in Larissa. His first book was a collection of poems titled Οι γάτες του ποιητή Δ. Ι. Αντωνίου (The cats of the poet D. I. Antoniou, 2012). Since then, he has published several books of short stories and micro-fiction, including Ιστορίες του Βαρθολομαίου Ολίβιε (The stories of Bartholomew Olivier, 2018), Ζαχαρίας Σκριπ (Zacharias Skrip, 2019) and Ιστορίες της Μάντσας (La Mancha Stories, 2020). His latest is the novella *Για να μην αποτύχουμε όπως ο Μπιόρλινγκ και Καλστένιους* (Let us not fail like Björling and Kallstenius) based on the real story of the ill-fated North Pole expedition mounted by the two Swedish naturalists.

Nikolas Koutsodontis (1987) is a Greek poet and literary translator. He studied sociology at Panteion University in Athens and is the author of two collections *Χαλκομανία* (Decalcomania, 1917) and *Μόνο κανέναν μη μου φέρεις σπίτι* (Just don't bring anyone home, 1921). His poems have been included in several anthologies, including *Ποιήματα της κρίσης* (Poems of the crisis, 2020).

Marilena Papaioannou (1982) grew up in the city of her birth, studied Molecular Biology and Genetics in Alexandroupolis and wrote her thesis in Geneva. Afterwards, she worked as a researcher in New York until 2013 when she returned to Greece where she has worked as editor and translator of biology textbooks, popular science books and scientific articles. Her first novel *Νικήτας Δέλτα* (Nikitas Delta, 2013) was shortlisted for the debut book State Award and *Reader* Magazine Award. Her second book is the novella Κατεβαίνει ο Καμουζάς στους φούρνους (Kamouzas coming down to the furnace, 2016) and her third Ένα πιάτο λιγότερο (One plate less, 2020).

Thomas Tsalapatis (1984) is a poet and playwright. He studied theatre at the University of Athens. His first poetry collection Το ξημέρωμα είναι σφαγή Κύριε Κρακ (Daybreak is slaughter, Mr. Krak, 2011) received the National Poetry Prize in 2012. His second collection Αλμπα (Alba, 2015) was published in French translation by Nicole Chaperon in 2017. His play Ανκόρ (Encore) was staged in Attis Theatre in Athens, directed by Theodoros Terzopoulos. The script and the poems of the performance were published in 2017 under the title Πνιγμός / Ανκόρ (The drowning/Encore). His third poetry collection is Γεωγραφίες των Φριτς και των Λανγκ (Geographies of the Fritzs and the Langs, 2018) and his latest Η ομορφιά των όπλων μας (The beauty of our weapons, 2021). His play Η Μόνικα Βίτι δεν θυμάται πια (Monica Vitti remembers no more, 2018) was presented at the Maison de la Poésie in Paris as a stage reading in translation by Clio Mavroeidakos and later staged in Athens and published. He has been writing articles for newspapers, magazines and web magazines since 2008 and has contributed to numerous anthologies and collections of essays.

SERBIA

Danilo Lučić (1984) graduated with an MA in Serbian Literature and Language from Belgrade's Faculty of Philology. He has published two poetry collections of poems, *Beleške o mekom tkivu* (Notes on soft tissue, 2013) and *Šrapneli* (Shrapnels, 2017). He writes articles and essays for several regional print and online publications. He was one of the organisers of the ARGH! poetry evenings, as well as an editor at Kontrast Publishing House. He lives and works in Belgrade.

Katarina Mitrović (1991) is a poet and screenwriter. She studied Serbian language and literature at Belgrade's Faculty of Philology and is currently a graduate student at the Faculty of Dramatic Arts. She has published two books of poetry *Utroba* (Guts, 2017) and

Dok čekam da prođe (While I wait for it to pass, 2018), as well as a poetic novel *Nemaju sve kuće dvorište* (Not all houses have a yard, 2020). She worked as a screenwriter on two TV series – *Grupa* (The group) and *Mama i tata se igraju rada* (Mum and dad are playing at work) – broadcast in 2019 and 2020 respectively. She is a co-writer of the short fiction film *Onaj koji donosi kišu* (The one who brings rain) directed by Isidora Veselinović and she also adapted the drama *Paviljoni* (Pavilions) by Milena Marković for a feature film directed by Dragan Nikolić.

Maša Seničić (1990) writes and works in the field of literature, film and media. She studied at the Faculty of Dramatic Arts in Belgrade, where she is now a PhD candidate. She has taken part in various local and international film, theatre, visual culture and poetry projects, workshops and events, while also contributing to film festivals as a writer, moderator and programmer. In 2015, Seničić won the prestigious *Mladi Dis* prize for unpublished manuscript, for her first poetry book *Okean* (The ocean). Her second book, *Povremena poput vikend-naselja (*As occasional as a holiday home) was published in 2019 and awarded the *Dušan Vasiljev* prize for best regional book. Her literary work has been published across the ex-Yugoslavia region and Europe, in magazines, anthologies and web magazines (*La Nouvelle poésie BCMS, Anthology of Young Serbian Poets, Kritična masa*, etc*).* She works as a freelance author and content creator, and is interested in exploring spatial and material boundaries of printed and digital material.

Nataša Srdić (née Miljković 1984) and **Srđan Srdić** (1977) are the literary couple behind Partizanska knjiga, the Serbian publishing house based in Kikinda, a town in the Vojvodina province near the Romanian border. Nataša graduated from the Department of

English Language and Literature, Faculty of Philology, University of Belgrade, where she also defended her doctoral dissertation *Scientific and Artistic Truth in John Banville's Fiction*. She is a literary translator from Serbian into English and vice versa with more than a dozen books to her name. Srđan Srdić is a novelist and short story writer, who founded the short story festival 'Kikinda Short' and edited a number of literary anthologies, including annual collections of work by authors appearing in the festival. His story is included here in Nataša's translation to represent her as one of the participants of Ulysses' Shelter project.

Goran Stamenić (1990) is a writer and translator, working in the fields of poetry and language experimentation and he explores poetic forms through mediums of translated texts, essays and music. His first poetry collection *Sveti magnet* (Holy magnet, 2016) deals with political uses of images and language. Since 2014, he has been teaching creative writing to younger writers. His poems have been translated into English, Welsh and German.

Vitomirka Trebovac (1980) was born in Novi Sad and graduated in Serbian language and literature from the Faculty of Philosophy of Novi Sad University. She is the author of three poetry collections *Plavo u boji* (Blue in colour, 2012), *Sve drveće, sva deca i svi bicikli u meni* (All the trees, bicycles and children in me, 2017) and *Dani punog meseca* (Full moon days, 2020). Her poems have been translated to several European languages. She is the co-owner of the Novi Sad bookstore Bulevar Books and the coordinator of the literary festival Sofa. She is currently working as an editor at the Bulevar publishing centre and is also engaged in various art projects in Serbia and abroad.

SLOVENIA

Dejan Koban (1979) is a poet, editor and poetry and media art event organiser. Among his other activities he publishes chapbooks presenting the poetry and prose of young, mostly unpublished writers from Slovenia and the region, and is one of the curators for the imprint *Sončnica, vsa nora od svetloba* (Sunflower, completely crazy from light) at Hiša poezije (House of poetry) in Ljubljana. To date he has published six collections *Tebi* (To you, 1997), *Metulji pod tlakom* (Butterflies under pressure, 2008), *Razporeditve* (Arrangements, 2013), *Frekvence votlih prostorov* (Frequencies of hollow spaces, 2016), *Klastrfak* (Clusterfuck, 2020) and *najbolj idiotska avtobiografija na svetu in izven* (the most idiotic autobiography in the world and beyond, 2020). He is currently preparing a book of collected poems.

Kristina Kočan (1981) is a poet and translator with PhD in contemporary American poetry and four collections to date are *Selišča* (Sojourns, 2021), *Šivje* (Stitchery, 2018), *Kolesa* in murve (Bicycles and mulberries, 2014), and *Šara* (Stuff, 2008). The end of 2018 saw the publication of her multimedia book s|prehod (pro|menade), which contains a selection of her poetry, audio recordings of poems set to music and photos by Bojan Atanaskovič. Her short fiction début *Divjad* (Wild game) was published in 2019. Her poetry is translated into more than ten languages and included in international anthologies, such as *Europe in Poems: The Versopolis Anthology* and *Other Words/Druge besede*. Kočan's translation work focuses on American authors. In 2021 she edited and translated an anthology of contemporary Native American short prose, *Po toku navzgor* (Upstream). As a songwriter she works with the Slovenian ensemble Brest with two acclaimed albums so far.

Davorin Lenko (1984) is a Slovenian writer, playwright and poet. He graduated in comparative literature from Ljubljana's Faculty of Arts and has published novels and two collections of short stories to date, including *Telesa v temi* (Bodies in the dark) as well as the Critic's Choice Award. The novel is available in German from the Slovene Writers' Association under the title *Körper im Dunkeln*. His second novel *Bela pritlikavka* (White dwarf) was published in 2017 and his third *Triger* (Trigger) in 2021. His collections of short stories are *Postopoma zapuščati Misantropolis* (Slowly leaving Misanthropolis, 2016) and *Psihoporn* (Psychoporn, 2020). In the spring of 2019, his monodrama *Psiho* (Psycho) was staged in Ljubljana to critical acclaim.

Tomo Podstenšek (1981) mainly writes prose fiction. He is the author of five novels, including *Sodba v imenu ljudstva* (The verdict on behalf of the people, 2012) and *Papir, kamen, škarje* (Paper, rock, scissors, 2016). His two collections of short stories are *Vožnja s črnim kolesom* (Riding the black bike, 2013) and *Ribji krik* (Fish scream, 2017). In addition to writing, he occasionally works in theatre and radio, as well as an organising literary events. He lives and works in Maribor.

Uroš Prah (1988) is the author of three poetry collections in Slovene: *Čezse polzeči* (Gliding over themselves, 2012), *Tišima* (Phush, 2015) and *Udor* (The blow, 2019). In 2018, he received the Exil Lyrikpreis Award in Vienna for his investigative poem 'Nostra Silva' written in German. In 2019 he was awarded a residency in New York by the Slovenian Ministry of Culture and in the Romanian National Museum of Literature in Bucharest by Traduki, in 2020 the IHAG residency in Graz, 2021 the Ulysses Shelter residency in Larisa, 2022 the residency at Literarisches Colloquium

Berlin. Translations of his collections, poems, and essays have been published in seventeen countries, most recently: *Silenci(e)mpuje,* Buenos Aires, 2022. He was the co-founder and long-time editor-in-chief of *IDIOT* magazine, program director of the international festival Literodrom, and the co-founder of the Museum of Madness, Trate. He is based in Vienna.

Ana Svetel (1990) graduated with a master's degree from the Department of Ethnology and Cultural Anthropology, where she is currently completing her doctorate and working as a researcher. Her poetry collection *Lepo in prav* (Fine and good, 2015) was shortlisted for the best debut of the year, and her book of short fiction *Dobra družba* (Good company, 2019) was shortlisted for the Novo Mesto literary award. Slovenian national broadcaster recorded a selection of stories from *Dobra družba* as a series of radio plays. Her second poetry collection *Marmor* (Marble) came out in 2022. She publishes poems and short stories in the leading Slovenian literary magazines (*Literatura, Dialogi,* and *Sodobnost*) and writes a monthly column for the Saturday edition of *Večer* newspaper. Her works have been translated into numerous languages and have appeared in various anthologies. She is included in the international poetry platform Versopolis. She is also actively involved in music and storytelling

Katja Zakrajšek (1980) studied comparative literature and is a literary translator from French, English, and Portuguese. She especially enjoys exploring less translated literary traditions and cultural spaces, and while she feels most at home with contemporary writing, she occasionally translates classics, such as Machado de Assis, *The Psychiatrist and Other Stories.* Her translations include writing from France (Marie Ndiaye, *Ladivine,* Nathacha Appanah,

Tropic of Violence), Senegal (Ken Bugul, *Riwan*), Congo (Fiston Mwanza Mujila, *Tram 83*), United States (Monique Truong, *The Book of Salt*), Brazil (Cristóvão Tezza, *The Eternal Son*, Adriana Lisboa, *Symphony in White*), and Great Britain (Bernardine Evaristo, *Girl, Woman, Other*) and she has also translated young adult literature (Clémentine Beauvais, *Piglettes*). She lives in Ljubljana and has stayed in various translation residencies from which she brings home ideas and shortlists for new translations.

WALES

Eluned Gramich (1989) is a German–Welsh writer and translator. She lived in Japan and Germany for several years before returning to Wales to pursue her PhD Creative and Critical Writing at Aberystwyth and Cardiff Universities. She has settled in Aberystwyth where she works as a librarian in the National Library of Wales. Her memoir about Hokkaido, *Woman Who Brings the Rain* (2015), won the New Welsh Writing Awards and was shortlisted for a Wales Book of the Year Award. Her stories have appeared in various magazines and anthologies, including *Rarebit: New Welsh Fiction* (2014), *New Welsh Short Stories* (2015), and the anthology of young Welsh and European authors *Zero Hours on the Boulevard: Tales of Independence and Belonging* (2019). Her non-fiction writing in English has been published in *Wales Arts Review*, *New Welsh Review*, and *World Literature Online*, and her writing in Welsh in *Pedwar o'r Gwynt*. Her translation of a short story collection by the Swiss author Monique Schwitter was published as *Goldfish Memory* (2015). Her debut novel, *Windstill*, is out in November 2022.

Steven Hitchins (1983) is a poet and poetry event organiser from Rhondda Cynon Taf in South Wales, who graduated with a BA, MA and PhD in English and Creative Writing from Aberystwyth University. His experience as a further education English Language and Literature teacher has formed a basis for the collaborative aspects of his poetry. His poetry is based on observing and working with the historical, geological and linguistic processes of his surrounding areas. His poetry has been published extensively in publications such as *Poetry Wales* and *New Welsh Review*, and he edits The Literary Pocket Book, producing origami pamphlets of experimental poetry. He has collaborated with other Welsh and international poets and artists on a number of projects.

Lloyd Markham (1988) was born in Johannesburg, South Africa, and spent his childhood in Zimbabwe, moving to and settling in Bridgend, South Wales, where he still lives. He graduated with a BA in Creative Writing from Glamorgan University (now University of South Wales), followed by an MPhil. His debut novel *Bad Ideas\Chemicals* (2017) won a Betty Trask Award and was shortlisted for Wales Book of the Year. 'Mercy' was included in the anthology of young Welsh and European authors *Zero Hours on the Boulevard: Tales of Independence and Belonging* (2019). In 2019 he received a bursary from Literature Wales to work on his second book, provisionally titled *Fox Bites*. During his residential stays in Ljubljana (Slovenia) and Larissa (Greece) he worked on a spiritual follow up to his debut novel – a darkly comic murder-farce set in a corner shop during a pandemic-struck Christmas Eve.

Grug Muse (1993) is a Welsh-language poet and essayist from Dyffryn Nantlle in North Wales. She studied politics at the University of Nottingham and in the Czech Republic, and did postgraduate research on Welsh travel writing at Swansea University. She is one of the editors and founders of *Y Stamp* literary magazine and press. Her second poetry collection, *merch y llyn* (girl on the lake, 2021) won the 2022 Welsh Book of the Year in the poetry category. Her work is published in both Welsh and English language publications such as *The Guardian*, *The Letters Page*, *O'r Pedwar Gwynt*, *Poetry Wales*, *Panorama: the journal of intelligent travel*, and in anthologies *Just So You Know* (2020) and *Y Gynghanedd Heddiw* (Cynghanedd today, 2020). She was also one of the contributing editors of the essay collection *Welsh (Plural)* published in 2022.

Morgan Owen (1994) is a poet and writer born and raised in Merthyr Tydfil who now lives in Cardiff. In 2019 he published a pamphlet of poems, *moroedd/dŵr* (seas/water), which won the Michael Marks Award for Poetry in Celtic Languages. The same year, he published a volume of poems, *Bedwen ar y lloer* (Birch on the moon). In August 2019, he won the Wales Literature Exchange/PEN Cymru Translation Challenge for translating poems by Julia Fiedorczuk into Welsh from their original Polish. In early 2020, he received a Literature Wales Author Scholarship to develop a collection of essays centred on Merthyr Tydfil. A poetry pamphlet, *Ysgall* (Thistles), came out in 2021.

Rebecca Thomas (1992) is a historian at Cardiff University, specialising in the history, culture, and literature of medieval Wales. She is especially interested in the construction of Welsh identity in medieval texts, and her monograph on this subject, *History and Identity in Early Medieval Wales*, was published by Boydell & Brewer in April 2022. She is also a writer of medieval historical fiction, and her first novel for young adults, *Dan Gysgod y Frenhines* (In the Queen's shadow) was published in 2022. This novel tells the story of Angharad, an illegitimate daughter of the Welsh king Hywel the Good, and recreates the most important political events of the tenth century through her eyes. In 2021, Rebecca's essay on landscape and names in South Wales, 'Cribo'r Dragon's Back' (Crib Notes on the Dragon's Back) won the inaugural essay prize launched by the Welsh-language cultural magazine *O'r Pedwar Gwynt*, sponsored by the Coleg Cymraeg Cenedlaethol, the national institution for Welsh-language education.

Notes and acknowledgements

The editor would like to thank the Ulysses' Shelter project participants and partners who supplied English-language translations of texts by the following authors, and all the authors and translators for their permission to use translations of their work in the anthology.

Krokodil: Danilo Lučić, Katarina Mitrović, Goran Stamenić, Maša Seničić, Vitomirka Trebovac

Sandorf: Maja Klarić, Dino Pešut and Maja Ručević

Slovenian Writers' Association: Kristina Kočan, Tomo Podstenšek, Ana Svetel, Uroš Prah

Thraka: Iakovos Anyfantakis, Filia Kanellopoulou, Nikolaos Koutsodontis, Marilena Papaioannou, Thomas Tsalapatis

Filia Kanellopoulou
The poems were written during her Ulysses' Shelter residency in Belgrade.

Marilena Papaioannou
'The tale of a pandemic' was written during the Ulysses' Shelter project as a result of one-to-one discussions with Eluned Gramich.

Maša Seničić
The poems were written in English for various projects.

The italics in 'Tiny rampant beasts' represent documentary material, gathered from different online media and reflecting what has been happening in the previous year on some of the European borders. This concrete information relates to the Hungarian hunters.

'Budapest' was previously published in *Budapest*, a photo-zine, with photographs of Nemanja Knežević (self-published in 2016, designed by *Metaklinika*).

'A heavy black cloud' was previously published in the artists' book *There are still some stones to carry*, made during MultiMadeira 2016 residence programme, in collaboration with Ana Konjović, Nemanja Knežević and Katarina Šoškić. Background: In 1418, two captains under service to Prince Henry the Navigator, João Gonçalves Zarco and Tristão Vaz Teixeira, were driven off-course by a storm to an island which they named Porto Santo (holy harbour); the name was bestowed for their gratitude and divine deliverance from a possible shipwreck by the protected anchorage. The following year, an organised expedition, under the captaincy of Zarco and Vaz Teixeira, was sent to this new land, and along with Captain Bartolomeu Perestrello, to take possession of the island on behalf of the Portuguese crown. Consequently, the new settlers discovered *'a heavy black cloud suspended to the southwest'*, which when explored they discovered the larger island of Madeira.

'That land, it doesn't exist' was written in July 2019, in Nicosia, Cyprus, during a programme Literary Line Cyprus – Balkans, as a part of the European project Reading Balkans.

Srđan Srdić

'About a door' was previously published in English in the short story collection *Combustions*, Glagoslav Publications, Belgrade, 2018. It is included here to showcase the work of translator Nataša Srdić who participated in the Ulysses' Shelter project.

Uroš Prah

Poems from collection *Udor* (The blow); untitled poems are listed with their last line.

Katja Zakrajšek

The essay 'Between 'Them' and 'Us' was written in English for the anthology.

Eluned Gramich

The story 'Something beginning with' was written for the anthology.

Steven Hitchins

The texts were previously published in *Canalchemy: The Larger Kilns*, Aquifer Press, 2019.

Lloyd Markham

'Locked in/Loose screw: a creative mistranslation', is an adaptation of Aljoša Toplak's short sci-fi story 'Into the Realm of Square Circles', written and recorded as a result of Lloyd Markham's residency in Ljubljana and its sound version can be found online: https://www.youtube.com/watch?v=jGuGI5DyMbk

Morgan Owen

The poems were written during his Ulysses' Shelter residency on Mljet.

Rebecca Thomas

The essay 'Crib notes on the Dragon's Back' was originally published in Welsh as 'Cribo'r Dragon's Back' by *O'r Pedwar Gwynt*, volume 17 (2021) and online:

https://pedwargwynt.cymru/cyfansoddi/cribor-dragons-back

PARTHIAN *Non-fiction*

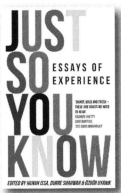

JUST SO YOU KNOW:
Essays of Experience
Edited by Hanan Issa,
Durre Shahwar & Özgür Uyanik

'Smart, bold and fresh – these are voices we need to hear' – Darren Chetty

£9.99 • Paperback • ISBN 978-1-912681-82-2

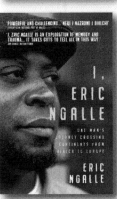

I, ERIC NGALLE:
One Man's Journey Crossing Continents from Africa to Europe
Eric Ngalle

'Powerful and challenging... neki / nazromi / diolch!' – Ifor ap Glyn

£8.99 • Paperback • ISBN 978-1-912109-10-4

WALES: ENGLAND'S COLONY?
Martin Johnes

Wales Arts Review Book of the Year

'An engaging and thought-provoking book' – Ifan Morgan Jones, Nation.Cymru

£8.99 • Paperback • ISBN 978-1912681-41-9

PARTHIAN *Non-fiction*

SEVENTY YEARS OF STRUGGLE AND ACHIEVEMENT:
Life Stories of Ethnic Minority Women Living in Wales

Edited and Selected by Meena Upadhyaya, Kirsten Lavine and Chris Weedon

Foreword by Julie Morgan and Jane Hutt. Introduction by Professor Terry Threadgold

'If you are looking for a book to inspire, then look no further.'
– Katherine Cleaver, Nation.Cymru

£20 • Hardback • ISBN 978-1913640-94-1

AN OPEN DOOR
New Travel Writing for a Precarious Century
Edited by Steven Lovatt

The history of Wales as a destination and confection of English Romantic writers is well-known, but this book reverses the process, turning a Welsh gaze on the rest of the world.

'If the mountains secluded Wales from England, the long coastline was like an open door to the world at large.'
– Jan Morris

£10 • Paperback • ISBN 978-1-913640-62-0

REFUGEE WALES:
Syrian Voices

Edited and selected by Angham Abdullah, Beth Thomas and Chris Weedon

Real life stories of Syrian people who have found refuge in Wales.

£20 • Hardback • ISBN 978-1-914595-30-1